The Journal of Levi Broas

Volume I

New York to Michigan
1837 - 1838

by L. Broas Mann

ISBN 978-1482303612

First Edition 2013

1 2 3 4

The cover picture, "Pittsford on the Erie Canal, 1837," is a painting by George Harvey and is the property of the Memorial Art Gallery of the University of Rochester, NY. I appreciate the help of Kerry Shauber and Jessica Marten in obtaining permission to use it.

To my beautiful wife Marion
and to the wonderful family she has given me.

Prologue

Levi Broas was the 18 year old son of Charles and Catherine Broas. With their older son Peter and daughter Sarah, they lived and worked on the farm of Charles' parents, Peter and Phebe Broas, near Binghamton, New York.

In the spring of 1837 Charles decided he needed to be on his own, so he resolved to move his family to Michigan.

Levi's Journal is his recounting of that move, written as he would speak it in the vernacular of the day.

*   *   *

Most of the people and places are a real part of the Broas family history, but the journal is a combination of fact, conjecture and imagaination.

Peter

The Town of Union, New York

Monday, September 26, 1836

I swear to God I dunno how he got down that far. We was fishin the Bradley up near Nanticoke when he stepped on a slimy rock. That creek moves pretty good, but it ain't that deep an Peter's a good swimmer – he musta hit his head on sumthin. He was all the way down into Nanticoke Creek an headin for the Susquehanna when those two dock workers saw him. He was near drowned by the time they fished him out. They dumped him on his belly an tried to pump the water outta him.

It was all my fault. He didn't wanna go fishin that day but I begged him til he gave in. I could always get Peter to do what I wanted. So after chores was done he got the rods an bait from the barn an we hitched Old George to the wagon an rode up to the Bradley. Fishin was good at first – we got two rainbow pretty quick. But then he spotted a quiet pool behind a fallen tree an started to wade downstream. That was when he slipped an fell. I tried to chase after him, but I fell too, an by the time I got up an outta the creek he was almost to the Nanticoke. I yelled "Peter! Get up! Swim!" But he couldn't hardly move his arms. He just kind of drifted with the current, round a bend an outta sight.

I ran along the edge as fast as I could, but the next time I saw him he was layin on the dock with those two guys workin on him. His face was awful grey. I knew right then he werent gonna come back.

An now I gotta tell Ma an Pa that I killed my big brother an my best friend.

God but I miss him! He taught me everythin worth knowin. Stuff like ropin an fishin an huntin. He even showed me where to hide in the barn loft that time Grampa Peter was gonna give me a whuppin for smokin corn silk.

It didn't matter to Peter that he was seven years older'n me. Now there's no one left here but Sarah, an ya can't fish or hunt or smoke with a girl!

The Decision

Friday, April 21, 1837, seven months later

Pa said it again, an each time he sounds more like he means it. We's leavin New York an goin to Michigan where goverment land is so cheap they're practickly givin it away. He says he needs to get out on his own in a place where a man can have lotsa land an do whatever he wants with it. Ma says it's really cause he can't get along with Grampa Peter, who runs the farm like we's all his hired hands.

I guess that's cause his Pa treated him like that. They was Dutch Quakers who come here from Holland, an moved from one place to nother round eastern New York every few years. They lived in Flatlands, Jamaica, Oyster Bay, Hempstead, New Paltz an a couple others. Guess they finally got tired a livin like nomads so they settled here in Union Town sometime after 1800 an been here ever since. Grampa Peter started farmin here an did pretty good at it. Course he had lotsa help -- at least seven kids. He was real strict an gave out the chores at breakfast every mornin, an if you didn't finish em you didn't get no supper.

So now Pa's talkin bout goin way out to Michigan. I'm kinda scared of travelin all the way to a wild place like that, but if we go through Detroit at least I'll get to see sister Rachel again. She an her husband Matthew an their baby Sarah Jane went to live near there couple years ago. That was hard nuff on Ma, but since young Peter died she cries most every night. An if she has to leave the rest a the family it'll be even worse. But once Pa has set his mind to sumthin he can get real stubborn bout it.

Saturday, April 22

What a brawl after supper last night!

Ma an Grampa Peter ganged up on Pa, tryin to get him to stay here on the farm. "Charlie, you got a wife an two kids to feed an all you know is farmin. You ain't smart enuff or man enuff to drag them off into that wild place on your own."

Pa turned beet red at that. "Old man, you can't tell me no longer how to live my life! If Cat an the kids want to stay here I'll go alone."

"Then you'll go alone," Ma said. "You wanna get yourself kilt go ahead, but you ain't takin me an the kids to hell with you." Everyone just stopped talkin an stared at her. She ain't never talked to Pa that way, least not in front of everybody.

Grampa got so angry he smacked Pa upside the head. If there was ever a chance they could change his mind that ruined it. Pa reared up like he was gonna hit back, but instead he just set his jaw an stomped outta the room.

Pa started packin up supplies for the trip an bout midnight he came back in an got us up -- me, Sarah an Ma -- an said, "I'm leavin at dawn tomorrow. Anyone wants to come better be ready."

After I went back to bed I could hear Ma an Pa talkin kind of soft-like. I guess they made up. He musta got Ma into changin her mind bout goin cause later she told me an Sarah to pack up what we wanted to take. We was all goin with him.

The Journey

Sunday, April 23

It was still dark when Ma drug me outta bed, but by then everyone else was up too. After breakfast Ma, Sarah an me said goodbye to Grampa an Gramma. Pa gave Gramma a big hug but just walked out like he didn't even know Grampa. We put our stuff in the wagon, hitched up Queeny, tied Old George to the back an started off just as the sun was lightin up the hill tops.

Pa reckons its bout 70 miles to Syracuse where we can pick up the Erie Canal. There ain't much more'n wagon trails an Indian paths a lot of the way so it'll take at least two or three days if we don't have no trouble with the horses or the wagon.

Monday, April 24

Well, that didn't work out too good.

We started out goin the same way me'n Peter had taken to go fishin last year – the day he got drowned. I didn't bite my stupid tongue fast enuff an when I let it blurt out, poor Ma got to cryin again.

But the real trouble was the mud. They was creeks an runners everywhere you looked, an in some places the trail was just soggy ruts. We'd loaded the wagon with everythin we could get in an it got stuck so much that Queenie an Old George was plum wore out time we'd gone 10 miles. Pa looked like he was bout to have a heart attack so Ma told him to find a place to rest while we made camp for the night. Sarah an me pitched the tent an got a fire goin, an Ma cooked up some mutton an beans.

Bear Country

Growin up on a farm you get used to the noises farm animals make as they move round at night. But it's different out here. Everythin is strange an kinda scary cause some a these noises I ain't never heard fore.

Pa said "Don't let the fire go out – it'll keep the foxes an coyotes away." So I got up every couple hours to add wood. That's when I seen it -- flames dancin in two eyes up on the hill. They was bout six inches apart an three feet off the ground.

That weren't no coyote!

Then I membered what Pa told me – this is bear country. I crept over to where he was sleepin an whispered in his ear. "Shh! I think there's a bear up that hill!" Pa's a light sleeper an right away he knew what I was sayin. He rolled over slow an got the loaded Kentucky that was always within his reach. Even a couple hundred yards away, Pa's a dead shot with that old rifle. I'd bet he prizes it moren us.

I pointed up the hill next to a big poplar an Pa saw it right away. Still lyin flat on his belly, he drew a bead on those eyes as the bear started to shuffle toward the camp. Just then Sarah woke up an saw the bear too. She screamed just fore Pa pulled the trigger. That threw off his aim enuff so the shot caught the bear in the shoulder steada the head. Pa's gun had been re-bored to .50 caliber an that big slug musta slammed the bear pretty good cause he spun halfway round an kinda lost his balance. Thank God for that cause it gave Pa time to reload fore the bear figgered out what he really wanted to do.

Now let me tell you, if you ain't never been charged by a angry bear, you don't know how scary it can be. That beast reared up on his hind legs an roared like a banshee. Then he dropped back on all fours an came crashin through the brush, hell-bent for our camp. (Got to admit, I wet my pants.)

But this is where I saw th'other side a Pa's temper. Cool as ice, he finished reloadin the Kentucky an took aim. By now the bear was only bout twenty yards from the fire, with Sarah an me next to it an that animal chargin right at us.

This time Pa didn't miss.

Tuesday, April 25

So much went wrong yesterday that today had to be better. The ground was drier an not so hilly. Glad I had talked Pa into bringin Old George along to spell Queenie. That horse was kinda stupid but with a lotta yellin an coaxin, the two of em got us bout another thirty miles.

We probly coulda gone farther today but we saw a old shack with smoke comin from the chimney an Pa decided to ask bout the rest of the trail north. He started to walk up to the door when the muzzle of another Kentucky came pokin out the window an a voice yelled, "Stop or I shoot."

Well, Pa sure nuff stopped. He backed up a few steps, set his rifle on the ground an yelled back. "Hey, wait a minute. We don't mean you no harm! Me an my family's tryin to get to Syracuse an just wondered if we could camp somewhere round here for the night."

The gun disappeared an the door opened. What was standin in it was somethin like I ain't never seen afore. He musta been pushin seven feet -- had to duck to get through the door. Looked like he was wearin a bearskin fer clothes, his feet was bare an his shaggy hair hung down over his shoulders.

When he saw me an Ma an Sarah an them two worn out nags he probly knew we wasn't no threat. He was still carryin the Kentucky, but it was pointed down at the ground. That's when Pa walked up a few steps an said, "We's tryin to get to Michigan where my other daughter lives. We figgered on takin the Erie Canal to the big lake an then find a boat that'll carry us to Detroit."

At that the big man laid down his rifle an shook hands with Pa. "I'm Rufus – sorry to poke the gun at you but lately they's been a few roughnecks come through here. Can't take no chances. I dunno much bout the big lake but you got bout 30 miles of tough goin tween here an that canal. If you wanta stick around a while I can tell you some things to look out for."

"We was hopin to camp round here anyway," Pa said, "so yeah, I'd like to hear anythin you can tell me. I shot a bear last night an we took some a the meat. Thought we'd try cookin it fore it spoils. Want to join us for dinner?"

"Sounds good, but if you ain't cooked bear meat afore mebbe you should let me do it. If you don't do it right its mighty tough."

Well that was one of the best meals I ever ate. Rufus soaked that meat in somethin pretty strong, then roasted it on a grill he had in his fireplace til it was tender n juicy. Ma watched everythin he did case Pa ever killed nother bear.

Over dinner Rufus got to tellin us how he come to be livin all alone in those woods. "Bout twenty years back my Pa got fed up with city life an thought he'd try huntin an trappin. Trouble is he didn't know nothin bout neither one, so we damn near starved. Then he tried stealin horses. Did pretty well too til some rancher caught him. They strung him up in the nearest town square. Had a good crowd watchin too. "

"The next year Ma up an died so that left me to figger out how to get along by myself. By then I'd learnt a thing or two bout trappin, an in these woods theys a lotta critters that make good eatin if you know how to cook em. But I near kilt myself coupla times figgerin that out."

Me an the women was pretty tired by then so we turned in but Pa an Rufus stayed up half the night talkin bout the way up to Syracuse.

Wednesday, April 26

Rufus fixed up a great breakfast. Then he said if we stick to the way he told Pa we'd oughta get there today. Well, he sure knew them woods cause we made it just like he said. We camped outside a town an'll go in come mornin.

Thursday, April 27

Syracuse

Finally – a town, but what a town! Buildins an people stead a trees an snakes. Roads steada trails, but honest, the roads ain't much better cause this place was built on swamp-land. Some places the mud is so deep men tuck their pants inside their boots. Ma an Sarah had to hike up their skirts.

An the smell! Under all that swamp is the biggest salt fields in the country an they really stink! They's acres of the stuff just layin in the sun so it dries out an then they shovel it up by the ton.

To ship the salt to market they bilt a railroad smack-dab through the center a town, so the soot covers everythin for blocks around! Then they put a park there an called it Vanderbilt Square. Why a guy with his dough would want to have such a filthy place named after him stumps me.

An as if that ain't bad enuff the place is full a hoodlums – robbin an beatin people, stealin from stores an even churches! They don't have enuff real law people yet so the place just kinda runs wild.

This mornin a punk come up an stuck a shiv in front a Pa an said "Gimme all yer money." Quick as lightnin Pa grabbed his wrist with one hand an his elbow with th'other. He snapped that arm so hard over his knee you could hear the bone crack. Bet the bum will think twice fore he tries that again.

So we figgered we couldn't get outta there fast enuff. Pa went to the general store an asked bout where the Canal dock is. The owner told him an said we had a couple hours til the next boat leaves.

He also told us we couldn't take horses or a wagon with us on a passenger boat. Guess we shoulda known that fore we left home, but it was still tough to hear. Old George was older'n me an had been a big part a the family. So Pa asked the store man for a place that traded in that kind of thing. He told us to try Markham's Livery Stable next to the canal dock. Well, we knew right then that we wasn't gonna get a very good price from a guy that had his customers in a hard place.

Back home Old George an Queenie woulda fetched bout $75 each, an everythin includin the wagon was probly worth almost $200. But old man Markham was shrewd. He made deals with a lotta folks like us who are forced to sell stuff they couldn't take on the boat. If he'd had enuff time Pa probly coulda got the price higher but after some arguin they blew the 20 minute whistle for the canal boat an he had to settle for $130.

The Erie Canal

The Boat

An there was another sight we ain't never seen the like of. They called it a "packet boat" but it looked more like a floatin cigar. It was over 70 feet long an kinda skinny cause two of em had to fit tween the tow path an th'other side a the canal.

Fore we could get on the boat we had to buy tickets. There was a big poster on a shack where a old guy with a long beard collected fares. The poster said the cost for one person was 1 cent a mile unless you wanted meals too. Then it was 1½ cents. An it showed the number a miles tween the different stops along the way. Sister Sarah's had more schoolin than me and is real quick with numbers. She come up with 190 miles from Syracuse to Buffalo. Then after a few more minutes of figgerin she said that come to bout $11.50 for four people if we wanna eat. Seein's how it'll take at least four days, Pa thought we should let em feed us so he paid the old man for that.

We walked over to the canal an there was this funny lookin boat. It was painted white with a row of windows on each side. The top was kinda flat cept it was curved a little from the middle to the sides, so rain could run off. People was sittin up there on benches. They was bout five feet bove the water so they got a pretty good view of what was goin on. At the front and back there was steps goin down to a lower deck, an then more steps goin into a long cabin.

Pa asked a guy what we could do with all the stuff we'd been carryin in the wagon. He took us down into the belly of the boat where there was stacks a bags an boxes. "Just put em on top a this stack, but make sure you got yer names on em. An watch what people getting off the boat afore you is carryin, cause some might try to steal yer stuff."

When we finished that we helped Ma and Sarah get settled in the women's section. Near the front a the boat in the main sleepin part was a sign that said "Ladies Saloon" an a big curtain hung across from one side to th'other that closed it off at night. Durin the day the inside a the boat was one long room with benches all along the sides and tables for eatin or readin or just sittin and talkin.

After we saw the women was settled in, me and Pa went up top to watch the boat take off. On the left side of the canal was a sorta street, with a buncha stores. There was lotsa people shoppin or just standin round watchin the boats. On th'other side was a path for the horses to go on when they was pullin the boat. They was huge animals with big hoofs cause they had to dig into the dirt to pull that load. An when it rained in some places they was sloggin through thick mud.

A few minutes after the Cap'n shouted "All aboard!" the two horses that was roped to our boat started to move it. At first, the boy guidin em had to tap their rears now'n then to keep em goin but they soon got the idea and kept the rope tight. But it was devlish hard work an I asked one a th'other passengers how long they could keep it up. He said the canal company keeps fresh horses in some a the towns and they switch teams every now'n then. He told me that most horses can't last much more'n a year or two doin that kinda work. The lucky ones are turned out to pasture but most are slaughtered for animal feed. Some folks are tryin to get laws passed that'll end that kinda practice, but they ain't had much success gainst the big companies that use the canal.

I was sure glad Pa didnt hear all that. Knowin it might be what happens to Queenie or Old George woulda tore him up even worsen it did me.

We drifted along, goin past farms and houses with people wavin at us from the shore, real friendly like. Then one of the crew told me some of em wasn't bein friendly at all. They was wantin us to not be there cause a what the canal did to their property. It cut right through their land, splittin some farms in two with no way to get from one part to th'other cept to go miles up or downstream to the nearest bridge. I felt kinda bad for em but then Pa said the canal done good for a lot more folks than it hurt. He said its called progress an there ain't no way to stop it.

There ain't many bridges but they're real low to the water – so low that the boats only clear by coupla feet. Everytime we come up to one a crewman yells "Low Bridge" an everyone on the deck has to duck down quick. He told us bout the time a young girl didn't duck fast nuff and got her head knocked real hard. She lost a good chunk a her scalp.

After bout a hour I saw nother boat comin our way round a curve. I wondered how they could pass cause both sets a horses was on the same tow path. But then the guide boy for th'other boat stopped his horses. His boat kept driftin so the rope dipped into the water and sank down nuff for our boat to pass over it. I figgered that was pretty neat, specially when our horses high-stepped over th'other guys rope.

Now we know why it was so cheap. They called it dinner but what was served sure weren't nuthin like Ma cooks. It was a kinda watery stew, stale bread an weak coffee. Some folks thought it was pretty good, so mebbe they were used to that kinda food but we ate better'n that on the trail! Made me think we don't preciate Ma like we oughta

When dusk come on they put away all the tables in the cabin. The row a benches along the wall was made into one a three rows a bunks and th'other two was swung down from the wall on ropes. They was so close together you bumped the guy on top whenever you turned over. That made for some squabbles in the middle a the night. They closed off the Ladies Saloon so I dont know how that was done, cept I heard some chatterin there too.

Friday, April 28

Well that was one heckuva night. Tween snorin and coughin and bumpin it was well nigh impossible to sleep. I sure do miss Grampa's farm now, spite a his ornery moods.

The Locks

Breakfast werent no better'n dinner so we didnt waste much time there. We wanted to get up on deck to watch goin through the locks. The Cap'n was tellin folks that for a few miles west a Syracuse is the only place where the locks take us down stead a up. Thats cause we was between the big rise from Albany, bout 400 feet, and another one bout 150 feet all the way to Buffalo.

When we started into the lock at Port Byron one a the crew unhooked the horses' rope from the boat and tossed it up on the path where the tow-boy picked it up. At first it seemed like we was goin to keep driftin right into the big gate in front of us, but then he took hold of another rope and jumped onto the wall close by. He quick wrapped that rope around a big pole buried in the wall and the boat stopped driftin just short a the front gate. Then he unwrapped the rope and began pushin on a big lever that opened nother gate buried in the wall behind us. It swung round and closed the backside so now we was in a big box fulla water.

Then there was a lotta grindin an whooshin as the water got pumped out, and we sank down bout a dozen feet to the bottom a the box. While we was doin that the horses was walkin down a hill on the tow path. Finally all the noises stopped. The gate in front of us opened an the boy tossed the horses rope to the crew man and we was pulled back out onta the canal an kept goin ahead.

Pa lit up his pipe and watched the horses like nothin special had just happened. But Ma and Sarah was kinda spooked by our boat bein pushed round like a big cork. I was too, but course I had to look like it weren't no big thing.

Ruth Ann

Sunday, April 30

Today we docked at Rochester to change horses an I figgered to take a walk round town. I was bout to step off the boat when I seen this family comin up the gang-plank, so I moved back outta the way. An thats when I saw her. They was four of em – Ma, Pa, a young boy an a girl so pretty I ain't never seen the likes afore. She stepped off the gang-plank onta the deck, smiled at me an said "Thank you." I ain't never gonna ferget that smile. I got all mixed up and mumbled "Sure – uh, yeah -- I mean yer welcome." I couldnt believe we was all gonna be on that boat together, mebbe even all the way to Buffalo! I decided not to go into town after all.

This evenin after dinner we was sittin on the deck, sposed to be watchin the farms and the towns go by, but I kept sneakin looks at that pretty girl. She looked bout my age, but you can never really tell with women. Her dark hair made a frame round her white face an rosy cheeks. Her eyes kept changin tween green an blue, dependin on the light. I couldn't stop lookin at em.

Now Pa ain't always a grouch -- fact he can be real friendly when he wants to. He went over to the new family an said hello to the old man. They got to chattin an soon he beckoned for the rest of us to come over too. All the names was passed round but the only name that stuck with me was Ruth Ann. I swear it sounded like a church hymn.

Pa told us later that the parents was James an Ann Just an the son was Josiah. They come all the way from Ireland, and was headin for Michigan, just like us. Don't know how I'm gonna sleep tonight, knowin Ruth Ann's only a few feet away b'hind that curtain.

Monday, May 1

An I didnt – not hardly a wink.

Rochester has two locks that'll take us up bout 20 feet, an we was goin t'go through one right after breakfast. We been through leven since we got on the boat, but I still like watchin, so even tho it was rainin a little I went up on deck.

The boat was just driftin into the box when she walked up and stood a couple feet away from me. I guess I smelled her fore I seen her; it was kinda soft, like a small buncha lilacs. I don't member how long it took me to answer after she said, "Good morning, Levi." It sounded like she was singin a Irish song. I was fraid of sayin sumthin stupid, but after studyin my shoes for a time I got it out -- "Mornin, Ruth Ann. Ever been through locks afore?" Some speech, huh? Least I got her name right.

"No," she said, "this is my first time on the canal. We rode the train up from Albany cause Papa said the Canal boat was real slow. But he wanted to find out what the boat ride was like so we got on for the rest of the trip to Buffalo."

By now the lock was startin to fill up with water. The boat is so skinny that it was rockin back an forth cause a the waves. Ruth Ann was lookin kinda scared an she grabbed my arm to keep from fallin over. Well let me tell you, it was like a lectric shock went through me. Course I planted my feet real firm an she held on til we was at the top an the water stopped swishin.

When the boat finally steadied she let go and looked kinda embarrassed. "Sorry, I thought we might tip over!"

"Shucks," I said, "we was safe, but I sure didn't mind you hangin onta me." Another big speech! Then I worried that she might think I was bein too friendly. But she moved a little closer so our arms just touched. I couldn't believe what was goin on in my head.

Soon the horses was hooked up and we got back on the canal. I was feelin really brave so I asked her, "How did you get all the way from Ireland to Albany?"

"We came to New York when I was just a baby," she said. "We went to live on my aunt and uncle's farm in Orange County and Papa helped Uncle Michael work the farm. But after a few years he got tired of always being told what to do, so he decided to go out on his own." That sure sounded a lot like Pa and Grampa Peter.

By now we had reached the second lock and was driftin into the box. When the gate closed behind us an the water started gushin in, she took my hand. I weren't sure if she was scared again or just wantin to hold hands. Either way was fine with me.

I was feelin pretty good by then so I decided to show her I weren't some dumb hick. "This is the last lock were gonna see today," I said. "They ain't nother one til we get to Lockport some time tomorrow. They got five of em there, one right after th'other, just like a big stairway. An they'll take us up over 50 feet!"

She said, "That's fascinating, Levi! I'm sure glad Papa decided to get on the Canal boat at Rochester." Then she gave my hand a little squeeze, an I stopped breathin for a coupla minutes.

By nightfall we was bout halfway to Lockport an what a day this has been – probly the best I ever had! Ruth Ann an me spent most of it just talkin an gettin to know each other.

She said, "Tell me about yourself, Levi, and how you got to be on this boat."

"Ain't much to tell. Got mosta my book-learnin from the local school house. But Gramma Phebe taught me an Sarah the important stuff bout workin an livin in a family. Been helpin out on Grampa Peter's farm since I was big enuff to reach the hen's eggs. But then Pa got tired a bein bossed around so he's takin us all to Michigan where he can get his own land. When he told Grampa, there was a big row an Ma said she wouldn't come with him. But after everyone settled down she agreed an here we are.

"Now it's your turn, Ruth Ann. What got you here?"

"Well, of course, I helped out on my Uncle's farm too, but I was lucky to be able to attend all the grades at our county school. I've wanted to be a doctor for as long as I can remember, but the ads for medical schools say, 'Women Need Not Apply.' So whenever I finished my chores, I started hanging around at the local hospital. I wanted to learn all I could about nursing by watching the doctors, especially when they brought someone in with an emergency. After a while they started letting me do some things, like cleaning wounds and bandaging them. I found that I love helping people who are really sick or in danger of dying. One doctor said I was pretty good at it, and sometimes he would have me get people ready for surgery.

"But that all ended when Papa decided we would go to Michigan, and I was really upset with him for a while. He finally convinced me that there might be even more need for nursing in that wild place where there are hardly any doctors or hospitals. So here I am!"

I was already pretty sold on this girl, but that cinched it. An sides, I kinda like the way she talks all proper an such. Mebbe she could teach me some a that.

Tuesday, May 2

Lockport

They jumped on board just fore Lockport. They was two of em, kinda tough an scruffy lookin. One was tall an skinny with a beard an squinty eyes that kept shiftin round like he was lookin for somethin. Th'othern weren't so tall but big an husky with thick arms an lotsa pictures on em – tattoos, I guess they was.

They went up an stood at the fronta the boat but they wasn't watchin the canal or the farms we was passin. They was facin the rear and kept lookin at the people on the deck. Finally, the squinty one poked his pal and pointed at the Just family who was all sittin together near the back on the tow path side. Tattoo kinda ambled down the deck til he was behind em while Squinty walked right up front a the Mister and started talkin real nasty at him.

Me an Pa an Sarah had been standin near the Justs on th'other side, watchin all this when Squinty started pokin Mr. J. in the chest. He said loud nuff for us to hear. "You better pay up now, old man, or you'll be sorry!"

Mr. J. stood up an said, "Braddock said I could pay him when we get to Buffalo."

"Braddock changed his mind. He needs the money now and told us to get it."

"How do I know he said that? Did he give you a letter or something?"

"No, there ain't no letter. He just told us to get the money."

"Well I don't think I should give you anything without proof."

Just then, Tattoo stepped back of Ruth Ann an put a arm round her neck. He said, "You callin us liars? You better cough it up old man or this little beauty will get more than a sore neck!"

I'd been watchin all that an wonderin what Mr. J would do, but when Tattoo grabbed Ruth Ann my throat tightened up and I felt a rage build from my belly to my head. I looked at Pa and I could see it comin, just like when the bear charged us in the woods. Pa's face got real calm, but his eyes was cold as ice. He barely nodded at me and Sarah but we knew what he meant.

We started movin real slow like. I got behind Tattoo and stood quiet, while Sarah went up aside Squinty, put her hand on his arm and said, "Anythin I can do for you, big guy?"

Sarah ain't no hussy, but she's real pretty with a voice like silk. She got Squinty thinkin bout her steada Mr J. long enuff for Pa to move behind him. An that's sumthin you don't never want. Quick as a flash he pumped a fist into the man's spine an nother to his ear. Mr. J just stood there like he didn't know what to make of it, so Pa kicked Squinty in the back a the knee and he went down like a empty sack.

Now I'm pretty good size, an I swear by then I was mad nuff to kill a tiger. I punched Tattoo's kidney so hard he screamed bloody murder. He turned round lookin to kill me, but it made him let go a Ruth Ann, which is what I really wanted. He grabbed me by the neck but I reared up and drove my knee into where no man ever wants somebody else's knee. He doubled over, so I drove my other knee into his face. Judgin from the blood, I guess it broke his nose and knocked out a couple teeth.

Then some a the crew come runnin over to see what all the ruckus was bout. When Mr. J. said what had been done to him and Ruth Ann they picked up both them bums and threw em in the canal. Its a good thing they could swim, cause by then we had just got into the first lock and it was startin to fill up. They got tossed around by the waves an had to work pretty hard to stay afloat til it reached the top. They climbed out and stood there sputterin an shakin their fists at us, but everyone on the boat just laughed at em.

I was glad it worked out so good, an Mr J told Pa he was real grateful for our help. But I kept wonderin why he didn't do nothin to protect his daughter or hisself. Ruth Ann came over an gave me a big hug and said, "Thank you, Levi. You were wonderful! I hope we can get on the same ferry boat out of Buffalo." Knowin that we might still be together all the way to Michigan set me up high. But her Papa looked kinda fussed – I dont think he took kindly to that.

Then Ruth Ann went over to where Sarah was an they sat there talkin for a long time, I guess bout what had just happened, but it seemed like more'n that. I wondered if they was gonna be friends, an I really liked that idea.

Wednesday, May 3

Tonawanda

We was goin through the last lock fore Buffalo when my world fell apart.

I was in the cargo hold pickin up our stuff when I saw Ruth Ann in a dark corner. She was cryin. I went over and touched her shoulder an she told me her Papa had decided to spend a couple weeks in Buffalo. Fore they leave he's gonna look up Mr. Braddock to pay off the loan, but first they'll visit a cousin he ain't seen in a long time. He said Mrs. J an the kids would like that cause his cousin's family lives in a big house right on Lake Erie an they can swim an fish an meet lotsa new people.

I think the real reason he's doin that is to keep me and Ruth Ann from gettin too friendly. Pa had told us soon's we get to Buffalo we's gonna take a lake boat to Detroit. I know the Justs is goin to Michigan too, but its a mighty big place, an I don't know how I'm ever gonna find Ruth Ann there.

I couldn't hold it in no more. I said, "Ruth Ann, I know we only just met, but I gotta see you again." She said she wanted to see me too, so we made a plan. I told her we'd be stayin with my sister Rachel and her husband Matthew Coons near Detroit. I gave her their address and said she should write me a letter when they get settled in and I'd find her wherever it is. She jumped up and put her arms around my neck an I held her real close. Then she tipped her head back so I kissed her, soft and slow.

I never knew somethin that felt so good could hurt so bad.

Buffalo

Another crazy city – like Syracuse only worse. The streets where the Canal and the Lake Erie sailors meet are wild – saloons, dance houses an worse – an fightin all the time.

There was lotsa carriages lined up at the Canal dock an Mr. Just picked one that would take them to his cousin's home. Fore they left, he thanked us all again for helpin em out on the Canal boat. While th'others got in the carriage Pa and Mr J. was out front admirin the horse, so Ruth Ann reached out the window and squeezed my hand. She said, kinda quiet like, "I'll write you as soon as I know where were going to be." Then they was gone.

I wonder if I'll ever see her again.

Lake Erie

The Michigan

The ferry boat docks was right near the Canal so Pa made us all go over together to buy tickets. There was so many nasty lookin people around that he didn't want us to separate. He was right, too. Three scummy lookin bums was watchin us from the dock an one of em come up to Sarah an tried to touch her. But Pa put one hand on his collar and th'other on the seat of his pants, picked him right off his feet and threw him in the gutter. Th'other two backed way off.

In front a the ferry dock was a big sign board that gave the times an prices for travellin to different cities on Lake Erie. Detroit was two or three days, dependin on weather and there was two kinds of tickets. The one they called Cabin was $8 a person an included meals an sleepin in a place with beds an furniture. Steerage was just cots to lie on the deck so it was only $3 each. For the four of us that only come to $12 stead of $32. Since meals on the Canal boat was so lousy, Ma figgered they wouldnt be any better here an said she didnt want to pay for that slop again. There was a store right near the dock, an with the savins she bought better food than we could get on board.

This is the biggest darn boat I ever seen. They named it the "Michigan," I guess cause that's where it was built, an it mostly runs to Detroit. It looks like its over 150 feet long an its got two big paddle-wheels on the sides. I reckon they's driven by a steam engine cause its called a steamboat.

But there's a funny thing – its got masts an sails too. Guess they're not too sure of the engine lastin all the way there'n back.

Thursday, May 4

The minute he got up this mornin Pa said he could tell that a storm was comin. Said he could feel it and smell it. An boy was he right! We was bout a day outta Buffalo an headin for the Port of Erie when the sky got real dark and the wind come whippin outta the northwest. The ship's rail is bout ten feet above water when its calm, but all of a sudden waves was crashin way up over it.

The Cap'n came up on deck an used a bull-horn to tell us Steerage folk to go down inside durin the storm. An he said they would make room for us to stay there tonight too cause we wouldn't make Erie til the next day.

Ma an Sarah went below but me an Pa stayed on the upper deck to watch the storm. It started to rain hard an the boat was really rockin so we grabbed onta the ropes that anchor the masts. Then a monster wave washed over us. My feet slipped out from under me an I lost my grip on the rope. When the boat tilted way over I slid down the deck an crashed into the railin. I let out a yell cause my left arm got twisted way round in back where it weren't ever meant to be. Pa let go the rope an slid down next to me just fore the boat started to right itself an tilt th'other way. He grabbed the railin with one hand an my leg with th'other an we kinda hung there til things leveled off. Then he said my shoulder came outta the joint, so he jerked my arm round in front again where it belonged. An if you ain't never had that done be very thankful cause it's a special kinda pain.

After all that Pa figgered we better go below. We saw Ma an Sarah sittin in a hallway in the Cabin class, lookin kinda envious of the folk goin in an outta their rooms. Pa was probly thinkin same as me – mebbe we shoulda spent the money so the women could be warm an dry.

They was sittin next to another Steerage family that was goin to Michigan too. Mr. an Mrs. DeGroot with their son Jacob an twins Willem an Johanna. Mrs. D was tellin Ma they'd been share-croppin on a farm near Buffalo. It was owned by a flinty old man named Simon Nordstrom who drove Mr D an all three kids real hard. But the worst part was he held back some a their share so they wouldn't leave the farm. Things got so bad they was thinkin bout quittin anyway, but one day while Jacob was roundin up the animals he got trampled by a horse gone crazy. Mr D tried to scare the horse off by yellin at it but that didnt work so he grabbed a pitchfork an stabbed it in the neck over an over.

Mrs D had trouble talkin bout Jacob, but she had to tell someone so she leaned toward Ma and said, "Mostly it was his legs got banged up, but he had lotsa bruises and scratches on his arms an back too. A doc come out from town an patched him up as best he could, but said he should be quiet for a coupla weeks. Then he took Mr D an me aside and told us the boy's knees got the worst of it. He said Jacob might not be able to walk so good no more, an he sure weren't goin to be workin the fields for a long time. When the owner heard all that he said he was gonna cut our share cause it was plantin time and we'd lost our best worker. Sides," he said, "you kilt my stud horse. He was worth a lotta money."

They stuck round til Jacob got used to the crutches an could move on his own, then packed up what little they had an left. She had a sister livin near Detroit and they figgered whatever that was like it'd be better'n what they was puttin up with in New York. But fore leavin, Andrew -- Mr D -- went up to the owner, grabbed him by the collar an said, "Gimme what you owe me Simon, or I swear I'll do to you what that wild horse a yours did to my boy."

Mrs D said, "Simon is crafty an crooked, but he ain't no fool. He knew Andrew would do what he said so he gave him the rest of our share. It weren't much but it'll help get us to Michigan."

That musta been when Ma decided the DeGroots was gonna be her special friends. She moved close to Mrs D an took her hand. They just sat there for a few minutes, then Ma started tellin her bout losin Peter an how it hurt just as much today as it did a year ago. An she said Mrs D was lucky that she still had Jacob even tho he was sorta busted up. By the time she finished they was both kinda teary but the woman smiled at Ma an thanked her for carin.

Friday, May 5

Erie, Pennsylvania

What a rough night! Thank God we was inside steada bein out on the deck. The ship was rockin round so much that people and their stuff was slidin back and forth in that narrow hallway. Ma got pretty sick, but she weren't the only one. Good thing there was a door on one side that opened to a outside walkway or it woulda got real nasty in that hall.

We made it to Erie this mornin an what a change! They got a harbor that's like a big circle with a long arm wrappin round an protectin it from the wind an waves. Soons we got into it everythin calmed right down. The town is tucked back in one corner. It ain't very big but it sure is busy. Cause a that good harbor they get lotsa business from all the ships comin an goin. An today everythin that floats was there, tryin to get outta the storm.

The Cap'n said we was gonna stay in Erie probly today an mebbe even tonight, dependin on the weather. But he said anyone wants to go ashore gotta be back by supper time cause we might leave by then if the storm lets up. Pa said it'd be good to be on solid ground an we should all go for a walk round the town. When we got off the boat Jacob was behind everyone cause a his legs, so Sarah said we should all go ahead an she'd stay with him an they'd just stroll around the dock area

I weren't sprised by that. She's been sorta cozyin up to Jacob since yesterday. Don't know whether it was cause she felt sorry for him or if she was takin a fancy. He's a pretty good-lookin guy, tall an husky-like, an he's bout Sarahs age. She's 20 an its bout time she found herself a man if she don't wanna end up a spinster. Too bad his legs ain't right, but mebbe they'll get better -- or mebbe it dont matter that much t'her.

Ma, Pa an me joined up with the rest a the DeGroots an walked a few blocks off the harbor. Ma and Mrs D found a grocery and bought some stuff we was goin short of. Pa saw a gun shop an went in to buy some powder for the Kentucky. What he had was in part of the ship's hold that flooded durin the storm and it got kinda wet. Mr D said he didn't have a rifle no more cause he had to sell it for cash to pay the doctor that treated Jacob.

Pa said, "Andrew, Michigan is a wild place. You can't go wandrin round there without a gun." Then Mr D said, "Can't be helped. After payin the fare for the boat I sure ain't got no money for a gun."

So Pa went up to the store owner and said, "Got any good used rifles? I want somethin cheap -- not fancy but works when you need it."

"Well, here's a old Tennessee flint-loader. You can see its kinda scratched and banged up, but it still shoots straight -- tried it just last week. Let er go for 50 bucks"

"Can't be worth moren 30," Pa said, "an I wanna try it first."

"Take er out back. If you like it I'll throw in powder an a box of shot – everythin for $40." Pa went out back where there was a target set up bout 100 yards away. He fired a few rounds an the Tennessee did pretty well so he came back in thinking he'd buy it.

Bout then Mr D spoke up. "Charles, I told ya, I ain't got $40. Hell, I ain't got $10!" But Pa came back at him, "Andrew, this is a loan. We're both headed for Detroit. I'm sure we'll meet up again an you can pay me back then. You gotta have a gun for huntin meat an for protectin yer family."

So thats how they settled it. Pa gave him the gun and ammunition, and Mr D gave Pa a note for $40 with a firm promise to find him and repay it. He carried that old rifle all the way back to the ship like it was a newborn baby.

When we got to the harbor I could see Sarah an Jacob just sittin an talkin. They was so wrapped up in their selves they didn't even see us comin. Pa looked at em an kinda frowned but he didn't say nothin.

Watchin them two made that ache for Ruth Ann come back worse'n ever.

Saturday, May 6

Just fore we sailed outta Erie last night us Steerage folk was told to go back on the upper deck. The storm had passed an the water weren't very rough, so me an Sarah went up an sat by the port railin. A full moon lit up the harbor an we watched the ship clear the breakwater an sail out into the lake.

 Ma an Pa didn't come up right away but was still on the outside walkway, right below us. They don't argue much no more – not since that big blowup at Grampa's last year. But this time they was goin at it, an we heard every word.

Seems Pa was upset bout Sarah gettin sweet on Jacob. He said, "The kid's nice enuff but with those legs he'll never get a good-payin job. An I won't have no daughter a mine marryin a guy who ends up on the dole or workin for a share-cropper. That's no life for my girl!"

Ma was quiet for a bit an I thought she was gonna agree. But then she came at him hard. "Ain't that just like a man -- ignorin the most important thing -- what *she* wants. If she gets much older without findin someone she'll be alone her whole life. An thats a lot worse'n bein married to a share-cropper!"

Bout now Sarah'd like to melt through the floor boards. She put her head in her hands and started to cry soft like.

I didn't hear no more from below after that. Then Ma came up on deck alone. She saw where we was sittin an knew right off that we musta heard em arguin. She came over an sat next to Sarah, took her hand an said, "Don't you fret bout what you just heard, honey. Your Pa'll come round."

"I hope so, Ma, because Jacob's a really good man. I know we just met but I can tell by the way he acts around his folks and the way he talks to me. Besides, what Pa says about him not being able to get a good job isn't so. His uncle in Detroit told Mr. DeGroot that both he an Jacob could start as apprentises in his machine shop. Even if Jacob's legs don't get any better, it won't matter there."

"That's real good, honey. An don't worry -- I'll handle Pa. Trust me." Sarah looked up at Ma and smiled. She said "I do Ma."

An that's when I figgered out somethin that had been botherin me for a long time. It usually looked like Ma took a back seat to whatever Pa wanted, like leavin Grampa's farm an comin west. But then I membered lotsa other times he'd take a hard stand on somethin, but later on seemed to change his mind. I guess she just worked her way quiet-like when they was alone.

Only this time she weren't so quiet.

Cleveland, Ohio

Cap'n says this lake whips up nasty storms without no warnin an he wants to be near land if nother one hits. So ever since leavin Erie we been huggin the shore, just out beyond the shallow water. We was bout halfway to Cleveland when it happened – the paddle-wheels stopped turnin an the ship just drifted toward shore. Then bout a dozen crewmen came runnin over to the masts an started hoistin sails. They was in a hurry cause we was getting closer to the shallow water every minute.

The storm had passed but there was still a wind outta the northwest so we couldn't sail straight. We had to wander back an forth to make headway – I heard somebody call it "tackin". It looked like real hard work cause them crewmen kept runnin their tails off movin the sails around. But they was good at it an we got to Cleveland fore dark.

There ain't no protected harbor here like Erie, but a river winds all through the shore land an it's quiet water, so we're gonna stay here for the night. Then some guy who had sailed Lake Erie a lot said the steam engine musta got busted an we was probly stuck here til they could fix it. Or else we could try to get to Detroit by sail, but it's a long way to go "tackin" gainst a headwind. Either way, he said it could take most of a week. That almost started a panic cause, lotsa folks said they had to be there by tomorrow night.

But then the Cap'n came out on the deck an said the engine was ok – we just used up too much firewood fightin that storm. He said we'd fill up here durin the night and take off for Detroit in the mornin. By time I woke we was back out on Lake Erie an the wind had died some. We had pulled away from the shore an were steamin straight for th'other end a the lake.

Sunday, May 7

I was too shook up an sore to write this last night.

We'd bout reached the place where the Detroit River dumps into Lake Erie. There's a map a that part posted on the wheelhouse an on the Michigan side it showed a whole buncha islands. Cap'n said he don't wanna tackle that river in the dark so we set to in a canal tween Horse an Edmond islands.

Bein Saturday, Cap'n said he usually has a little party fore we get into Detroit where most folks'll get off. So he invited all the Steerage people down to the Cabin meetin room where there's nuff space for everyone. One a the crew was playin a fiddle an there was a table with cheese an crackers an two kindsa fruit punch – one had a sign that said "Not for Kids!" Ma, Mrs D an the twins went down there an had a chance to say goodbye to friends they'd made. But Pa went back to the stern an asked the first mate if he could see the steam engine up close, so he took him down below. Sarah an Jacob decided it was a good time to be alone so they stayed topside sittin up by the bow talkin an lookin at each other like there weren't no one else in the world.

Pa had told Mr DeGroot that he should practice loadin powder and shot into the Tennessee in case he needed it in a hurry. So he figgered with most folk down below this would be a good time – sittin off by hisself loadin an unloadin the rifle til he got real good at it. I think he just likes holdin it an playin with it -- like a new toy.

I was sittin nearby watchin Mr D when two scruffy-lookin crewmen come wanderin' up to the bow. One of em seemed kinda familiar but I couldn't member where from. But when he moseyed up to Sarah it come back to me sudden-like. He was the one that tried to touch her back at the dock in Buffalo – the one Pa threw in the gutter. Only now, Pa weren't nowhere near.

This time he didn't just try to touch her – he grabbed her arm and pulled her up on her feet, sayin,"Yer ol man ain't gonna stop me this time sweetie, an neither is that busted up gimp." I tried to get at him but th'other guy grabbed me by the neck, kicked my legs out from under me an held me down.

Sarah yelled and pounded the bum's chest with her hands but he just hung on an started rippin her dress off. Jacob couldn't get to his feet quick nuff so he picked up one a his crutches an jabbed the guy in the back – hard. It made him let go a Sarah but then he turned round an pulled a big knife outta his belt. Jacob started crab-walkin backwards on his hands and feet but Scruffy was faster. He swung the knife an caught Jacob's leg, openin a vein an blood come pourin out. Jacob stopped movin an the crewman reared up high, raised the knife an looked like he was gonna swing it at his neck.

Mr D was runnin over to try to stop the fight but when he saw the man bout to kill his son he stopped cold. The Tennessee was loaded and cocked. He leveled the gun, aimed it at the crewman an fired. Scruffy's chest busted wide open an he dropped to the deck like a stone. Then Mr D swung the rifle around an aimed it at the guy holdin me down. "Let go a him or you get the same!" he yelled. The guy froze, then he turned an ran down the port side toward the stern. Guess he didn't know you can't fire a flintlock twice without reloadin it.

Pa had heard the shot and was comin up front along the port railin when they crashed into each other. He membered the guy from the dock at Buffalo an figgered he musta been part a whatever was goin on, but he just pushed him aside an ran on by. When Pa got to the front a the ship he stopped an stared at the mess --

- A bloody corpse on the deck.
- Jacob tryin to stop his leg from bleedin.
- Mr D holdin a smokin rifle and lookin dazed.
- Sarah with part a her dress ripped off.
- Me just sittin on the deck tryin to breathe.

"What the hell happened here, Levi?" I was tryin to tell him when the Cap'n came runnin up and asked the same thing. So I started over an told em both bout the wildest five minutes I ever lived.

Then the Cap'n went over an put a hand on Mr D's shoulder and said "Mr DeGroot it sounds like you did the right thing, protecting your son an all. But there's been a shooting on my ship and I've got to hear from everyone who saw any part of it. Meantime, I'll have to ask you to stay in my custody til I can hold a Captain's Mast. And I'll need to take your rifle too."

"Take the damn rifle but you ain't takin me til I see to my son." Sarah was tryin to use a piece a her ripped dress to bind up Jacob's leg, but she was cryin an shakin so much she couldn't tie it, so Mr D finished up. By now Sarah was feelin embarrassed with part a her dress gone. Ma had come up to see what all the ruckus was bout an when she saw Sarah shakin an tryin to cover herself she took her shawl an wrapped it round her. Then held her close til she settled down.

The Cap'n called some a his crewmen to pick up the dead man an fix him up for what they called "burial at sea," even tho it were just a lake. After that they swabbed the deck clean so there weren't no traces left a what went on there, least not what you could see. But us folk who was there that night will never forget what we saw.

Monday, May 8

Yesterday was different from any other day I ever seen. Seems like on board a ship the Cap'n is just a little bit below God. He's the minister, the lawman, the doctor an the boss of just about everythin that goes on. Bein Sunday the Cap'n held a short worship service on the upper deck. He thanked the Lord for gettin us to Detroit, asked for good weather, prayed forgiveness for Mr DeGroot for killin a man even tho it was necessary, then asked the Lord's forgiveness for the crewman what was committin the sin a lust an woulda murdered Jacob if Mr DeGroot hadn't up an shot him first.

After that we steamed back a few miles into the lake where the water was deep. Then we all stood round the port railin while the Cap'n said a few last words fore the dead man was slid over the side on a long plank. The weights they tied on his legs pulled him outta sight real quick.

Today was the Cap'n's Mast. He got everybody together who seen any part a yesterday's shootin an had Mr DeGroot tell what happened. When the Cap'n asked if anyone had a different view of it no one said anythin. Then Pa stepped up an said he wanted to thank Mr D for what he done cause it saved his daughter Sarah from sumthin awful. The Cap'n called the shootin just, gave Mr D's rifle back an dismissed everybody. After that we moved up river to the docks at Detroit where most of us would get off.

It's been 18 days since we left Union Town an a awful lot has happened durin that time. But the one thing that meant more'n anything else to me was meetin Ruth Ann Just. I'm sure hopin to meet up with her again, but Michigan is a mighty big place an I don't know where any of us is gonna end up. Right now we gotta find sister Rachel and her husband Matthew Coons so I can get the letter Ruth Ann promised to send there.

This was also time to say goodbye to the DeGroots. Mom an Mrs D had got kinda close so it was hard on them, but Sarah an Jacob was really hurtin. They was alone near the bow, their favorite meetin place, an he said "Sarah, I don't know what's gonna happen to us here. Mebbe the job in my uncle's machine shop will work out, mebbe it won't, but I do know I gotta see you again. Gimme your sister's address an I'll write to you soon's I know how things are goin here."

Now it ain't right for a girl to take the lead but Sarah couldn't help herself. She threw her arms around Jacob's neck an kissed him – hard. Then without a word she turned an ran into Ma's arms.

Detroit

Tuesday, May 9

Pa figgered the first thing we needed was horses an a wagon, not just to get to Rachel's but later when we go west. So he asked one of the crewmen if there was a livery stable nearby. He said there was two or three, an if we meander along the river front we should find one.

But after the trimmin he took in Syracuse, Pa was kinda leery bout spendin that kinda money to buy a horse from a stranger. So he asked the Cap'n if he knew a place where he could trust the owner. He said, "We're docked by the Merchant Wharf at Griswold Street, Mr Broas. Take that north a few blocks to State Street where you'll find Seymour Finney's livery. Tell him Cap'n Herman Schmidt sent you. You'll get a good horse and wagon at a fair price. I've sent people to him before, and have not heard any complaints."

So me an Pa walked up to the livery. We went right up through the middle a the city an it only took a few minutes. When we got to the livery there was some coloreds out front just millin round. They looked at us like they was kinda fraid, but we just walked right by em into the barn to find Mr Finney. He was talkin to another bunch a coloreds, gettin em loaded into a wagon. When the horse an buggy moved off he turned to Pa and said, "Sorry to keep you waiting. I'm Seymour Finney, what can I do for you?"

"I'm Charles Broas and this is my son Levi. We came from New York by the Canal an took the steamship "Michigan" across Lake Erie. Me'n my family's headed for my daughter's in Oakland County. Then we're plannin to go west to settle our own place. I figger I'm gonna need two horses an a good wagon. Cap'n Herman Schmidt said you'd give us a fair deal."

"Well, you can count on that, Mr. Broas. I've known the Cap'n for several years and respect his friendship."

Mr Finney took us over to the stable part a the barn an said to pick out horses an a wagon big nuff to carry our family an our belongins. There was lotsa horses there an Pa checked em all over, but he settled on a big roan named Mike that seemed kinda friendly. Mr Finney said he'd sell him to us for $70. There was a mare in the next stall an Mr. Finney said Maggie had been a mate to Mike. He said Pa could have both Mike an Maggie an a two-yoke wagon for $180. That were more'n what we got for Queenie an Old George in Syracuse, but Pa figgered it was still a fair price.

Mr Finney hitched Mike an Maggie to the wagon an just fore we left Pa asked him bout all the colored he saw round the place. "Well, Mr Broas, before I answer that I need to know how you stand on slavery."

"Mr Finney, I'm a Quaker. I may not be a very good one but I ain't never believed one man should own 'nother one," said Pa. "It just ain't right an never will be."

"Then you think like me. I'm a Quaker too, and I've been an abolitionist long as I can remember. These folks are runaway slaves, mostly families, trying to get away from their southern owners. There's a new law that says any owner that recaptures his slaves can take them back. And it says anyone helping a slave escape is commiting a felony, so you see why I needed to know your stand on this.

"This barn is the last stop on what we call the Underground Railroad to Canada. People in other states who think like us about slavery have been helping these folks get to Detroit. From here we take them up-river a piece where some other folks transport them across to Hog Island. When it gets dark enough a couple of young Canadian boys come and take them to Windsor.

"Mr Broas, you said you're a Quaker and that your son is named Levi. That's interesting because a Quaker named Levi started the Underground Railroad. Levi Coffin opened his home in North Carolina to fugitive slaves. Then he traveled to five or six other states and convinced more Quakers to help. We give escaping slaves food an a place to rest before helping them along to the next safe place. We hide them in attics, cellars, sheds, caves, secret rooms, or in barns like this. So we Quakers are committed to fighting slavery and helping those trying to escape it. Levi, you can be proud of that."

Well, that got me to thinkin bout the Quakers an wonderin why Ma an Pa never made much ado bout it. Mebbe that was nother thing where Grampa Peter set the rules. Anaways, we set out from Finney's Livery with a whole different idea bout slavery, an bout Detroit, too.

It was late afternoon time we got back to the ship, too late to head up north. Cap'n said he wasn't leavin Detroit til morning an we could stay aboard tonight.

Wednesday, May 10

Early this mornin, just fore we packed up the wagon, Pa asked Cap'n Schmidt the best way to get to Groveland in Oakland County.

"Groveland is between Pontiac and Flint, Mr Broas. The road that goes there was originally the old Sagainaw trail used by the Sauk Indians. It was important for the early settlers cause it was the only decent trail that went that far north."

"Where's this Sagainaw trail Cap'n?"

"Starts right here at the river, actually. In Detroit it's called Woodward and it goes straight up to Pontiac. The first couple miles in the city are pretty solid so it's easy going. But beyond that it got so busy that a few years back the Federal goverment made some of it into a plank road. They chopped down a lot of trees to widen it and then they laid the logs across the trail. In dry weather it's just a rough ride, but when it rains some of the logs sink into the mud. It's a big improvement over the old Sauk trail, but there's still a lot of rough spots, so keep a sharp lookout ahead of your team.

"Now when you get to Pontiac it's not a plank road anymore – just the old Sagainaw trail -- but stay on it and when you come to the Old Mill Road you're in Groveland."

We didn't have no map, so we just did what the Cap'n said. Long as we was in Detroit the road was fine so we had good travelin. But then we hit the plank road an it got pretty bumpy. The horses wasn't used to those logs an now an again their hooves got stuck tween em – they had to work pretty hard to keep goin.

This time of year the days is extra long an we musta been halfway to Pontiac fore it started gettin dark. Pa was lookin round for a place to camp when we saw a sign that said "Bagley Inn, Travelers Welcome." Now we knew right off it weren't gonna be cheap, but that's when Ma spoke up.

"Pa, we ain't slept under a decent roof since we left home. Even on that steamship we was out on a open deck with a buncha other people. I wanna stay in our own room for one night – right now!"

The Bagley Inn

Pa's a pretty smart guy. He knows when to argue an when to let go, so he pulled our wagon up longside all th'others an went inside. Guess he figgered he'd saved some money by takin Steerage on the steamboat, an now it was time to spend some. When he come back out he took Ma's arm and scorted her up the front steps with me and Sarah trailin behind. On the way in he said to her, "Now don't pay no mind to the way some of these folks is dressed up real fancy. Mebbe they live round here, but when they's travellin bet they don't look no better'n us."

Well, he was right bout fancy. An it was hard to pay folks no mind when they looked at us kinda funny. But Ma stuck her head up high an walked right on by just like she b'longed there.

Ma an Pa went up a stairway to the room but me an Sarah wandered round the lobby lookin the place over. There was a big board explainin bout the Bagley Inn so we stopped to read it. It said the place is only bout three years old an they copied a lotta stuff from the Tremont Hotel in Boston so it was real modern. They put in new gas lamps, plumbin, even a water closet in every room. I couldn't hardly wait to see that!

We was bout to go up when Ma an Pa came down an said we was all goin to eat in the dinin room. Right off, I took Pa aside an asked him bout the water closet. I ain't never seen Pa look embarrassed but his face got kinda red. He 'lowed bout how it didn't seem manly to use that contraption, but since there weren't no outhouse he didn't have a choice. But the way he said it I knew it were the end a that subject.

Just as we was goin toward the dinin room one a the fancy ladies sniffed an turned to her friends with a scowl on her face. "It seems as though they let *anyone* in here now," she said kinda loud.

Well, Ma like to fall through the floor. But then a well dressed man came up to the woman and said, "Mrs. Walton, I'm Judge

Amasa Bagley, the owner of this Inn. We have a firm policy – travelers may not be as well attired as local residents, but they are just as welcome." At that the woman got kinda red and turned away.

Then the judge came over to Ma and Pa and said, "Sir, madam, I apologize for the lady's poor manners. So you'll know I meant what I said about being welcome here, I want you to be my dinner guests. We would like to serve your family our special menu this evening with our compliments. Will you honor me by accepting it?"

Well, they couldn't talk for a minute. Then Pa blurted out, "Well, sure ...uh....I mean, yeah ...ok.....Mr ...er....Judge Bagley. Thanks, sir!'

Well believe me, that dinner was somethin I won't forget in a long time. Not cause people was glancin sideways at us – we just ignored em. But I ain't never ate vittles like that. I don't know what them dishes was called, but a man in a fancy suit brought em out one at a time stead a putting everythin on the table at once. He started with sumpin like what we feed the rabbits, but it was real tasty. Then he brought a kinda spaghetti only it was a funny shape an all smothered in a red sauce that didn't taste like anythin Ma makes.

We didn't see him for a while an I was wonderin if that was all we'd get. But then he come out with some meat that was kinda thick. Sarah asked what it was called but he answered her with a coupla words that sounded kinda French. I still don't know what it is but it was mighty tasty. He also brought a dish that musta started life as a potato but got changed a lot. An there was some fuzzy green stuff with a cheesy sauce all over it.

That was probly the biggest meal I ever had. I figgered to go for a walk to help things settle down when Mr Fancy Pants came out again holdin a big tray up high in one hand. When he reached up with th'other hand there was a big "whoosh" an flames jumped almost to the ceilin. I grabbed my water glass an was bout to dump it on the tray, but Sarah pulled me back down an said "Stop, Levi; that's Peach Flambe. It's supposed to burn like that." I know Sarah went to a different school from me but they sure musta taught her a lotta stuff I never heard of.

Well I tell you, that was a fittin end to a dinner I ain't never seen the like of. It tasted real good even if I didn't know what it was. Even Ma said it was the best meal she ever ate, an she was the best cook in Broome County.

Thursday, May 11

What a day this was!

It all started after breakfast this mornin when me an Pa went lookin for Judge Bagley so he could thank him proper for the feast last night. We found him out in the garden plantin tomatoes.

"Mornin, Judge. Seems like you wear a lotta hats round here."

"Good morning, Mr Broas, Levi. Yes, I enjoy keeping my hand in most of the operations at the Inn. As I'm sure you know, we pride ourselves on the food we serve here. This is a hybrid tomato that I developed several years ago and the only kind I allow in our restaurant."

"Well I just wanted to thank you for that dinner your people served me and my family last night. I don't recall we ever ate like that before."

"It was our way of apologizing for the unfortunate remark by one of our guests. Mrs Walton can be a nice lady in her own circle, but is a bit of a snob outside of it. I assume you're resuming your journey now, Mr Broas. Where are you headed, if I may ask?"

"Well, Judge, that's not real clear right now. I've spent my whole life workin for somebody else an last month I decided I had enough of it. They say the goverment is sellin land in the west part a the state real cheap, so I'm thinkin a gettin a stake out there. But my daughter lives somewhere north of here in a little place called Groveland, so we'll go there first, that is if I can find it!"

"I think I can help you there. As you know, you are on Woodward now and that will take you right into Pontiac. North from there it is no longer a plank road but more like an improved trail. Except if it's raining. Then there's nothing "improved" about it – it's just plain mud.

"After about 15 or 20 miles you should come to an old mill and that's in Groveland. Somebody there should be able to direct you to your daughter's home.

"I hope you and your family have a good trip, Mr Broas, wherever you end up. And if you get back down here on your way out west please stop in and say hello."

"Thanks again, Judge, we will. This sure is a great place. An mebbe next time you can be *our* guest for dinner"

Pa figgered the road couldn't be any worse than the muddy Indian trail we took from Binghamton to Syracuse, so he felt pretty good when we set out this mornin. It looked like it might rain so we put the wagon cover up so Ma an Sarah could stay dry. The goin wasn't bad up to Pontiac, cept when Maggie kept gettin a hoof caught tween them durn planks.

Pontiac is just startin to grow up. They got a general store where the nearby settlers can come to buy or trade for what they can't grow, an another place that sells farm equipment. An there's a inn for travelers to sleep, an it has a bar for eatin, drinkin an partyin. There was a coupla dancin girls standin out front, an when Ma saw that she said "Let's keep goin, Pa. I wanna get to Rachel's fore dark." So we just kept goin.

Soon's we left town the forest turned real heavy with big trees, an they say the rest a Michigan is the same way. The only way to get through it is on the creeks an Indian trails that run all over the place. Since we didn't have no boat we was stuck with the trails.

50

The Russells

We'd used up most a the mornin plowin through mud when I heard some little bells ringin up ahead. Next we saw three cows an a goat wanderin around lookin for anythin they could eat. Then I heard nother sound I know real well – a axe choppin wood. Round a bend in the trail we saw a buncha trees layin on the ground an in the middle of a clearin was a rough log house. Pa stopped Mike an Maggie to take a look-see. A skinny yellow dog came outta the cabin barin his teeth, growled low in his throat an started crawlin toward us. But a big man with a red beard put his axe down an said "Stay, Cropper, they ain't no harm to us."

Then he walked over to our wagon an smiled up at Pa. "Hi stranger. My name's Josiah Russell. Where you headed?" Pa gave me the reins and jumped down to the ground. "I'm Charles Broas an this is my son Levi. My wife Catherine and daughter Sarah are in the wagon. Right now we're goin to Groveland to see my other daughter," he said as they shook hands. "But then I'm figgerin to go west an buy some a that land grant property the goverment is sellin out there."

"You sure you want to take your family out there, Mr Broas? I hear it's even wilder than here, an lately there's been talk of a fever goin round."

"Well, that's my plan, but I'd like to learn all I can bout that part a the state."

"It's nearly noon. Why don't you an your family come in for dinner an we can talk some more?" An that's what we did.

The Russells was real friendly folk, specially the missus who made us feel welcome even tho we was suddenly dumped on her. Ma said "I'm Catherine Broas, Mrs Russell. I know men don't think nothin of it, but we shouldn't be imposin on you like this"

"Please call me Betsey, Catherine. It gets so lonely out here I'm just glad for the company. My oldest son, Amos, is married and moved to Flint, an the only creatures I see sides Josiah and William are bear and raccoon."

William, th'other son, was kinda handsome, I guess. He was bout Sarah's age, an mebbe that's why he looked twice when she got down outta the wagon -- an he was still lookin. I spose she was still fancyin Jacob DeGroot, but that didn't keep her from lookin back.

Dinner was real good, cured ham, fresh bread an goat's milk. Mr Russell was tellin Pa bout travellin to the western part a the state. He said the best way is to take the Grand River Trail that goes all the way to Grand Rapids.

"But the trouble with that, Charles, is gettin to it. There's a trail goes west from Pontiac through the wildest forest you'll ever see. We started to go out there last month but the rain made the mud so bad we gave up an came back. An the mosquitoes -- they come at you in clouds! You're so busy swattin you can't do nothin else. I heard last week there's a fever that came from the mosquitoes ragain round south a Grand Rapids down to Kalamazoo. It's the ague an it kills people. You sure you want to take your family out there?"

"Well, mebbe not Josiah. Right now we'll be stayin in Groveland for a while. Rachel an her husband, Matthew Coons, got a big farm an could use help workin it. I dunno how long we'll be there – least til he can get some other help. While we're there I'll try to find out more bout the land an the livin out west."

"That makes more sense, Charles. Once in a while a fur trader or a merchant on his way back to Detroit goes through here. They know where the best land is an how things are goin with the settlers out there. An they could tell you which Indians are more friendly, tho we ain't had trouble with any of em hereabouts."

While all this jawin was goin on Sarah and William was sittin at the other end of the table. They'd been talkin all through dinner an seemed to be gettin real friendly.

It was near onto middle afternoon an Pa figgered we should get movin. Mr R said we's only bout ten miles from Groveland but the trail ain't very good so it might take til supper time. We said goodbyes an thank yous with hand shakin all around. William took a long time lettin go of Sarah's, an I wondered if she was startin to forget bout Jacob DeGroot.

On the way back to the wagon I was walkin next to her but behind Ma an Pa, so I spoke quiet-like. "Kinda nice guy, that William, huh?"

"Yeah, he's ok I guess," she said.

"Changin yer mind bout Jacob?" I asked.

"I wouldn't say that, but there's something about William that's kinda different."

I snickered at that. "Well, yeah. He's got two good legs --- an a lotta other good stuff too!"

"I know," she said "but that's not what I meant. I got sort of a strange feeling while we were talking, like I didn't want it to end."

"Well, you better make up your mind cause I figger Jacob will be writin you some day soon."

Groveland

While we was at the Russell's Mike an Maggie got fed an rested so soon's we got back on the trail they was rarin to go. It was kinda rough but they just plowed on ahead. When Pa saw a man walkin down th'other side he pulled up an asked him if he knew where the Coons farm is. "Sure – just go east at Old Mill, then bout a half mile down you'll see a smaller road with a sign that says 'Matthew Coons.' Can't miss it!"

Well, we sure nuff missed it. Got bouta mile down Old Mill fore we turned round. Saw the sign on the way back, half broke an layin on the ground. Up that road a piece was a big old-fashion farm house with a porch all around an "Coons" carved into one a the posts. Pa guided Mike an Maggie into the yard an we all got down from the wagon. An then I saw somthin I ain't never seen fore an probly never will again. When Rachel came runnin out the back door both Ma an Pa started cryin like babies. The three of em hugged like it weren't gonna end.

But that weren't the half of it. Matthew came out carryin a baby girl on one arm an held her up next to sister Sarah. Then he said "Member little Sarah Jane, Ma? Back home when she was born you asked Rachel to name her for her aunt cause you thought they looked so much alike. Well, you sure was right. Now she's two an they look even more alike." Then Matthew handed her to Ma an she started to cry all over again.

After supper that's pretty much how the evenin went – family gettin requainted and little Sarah Jane in the middle of it all.

Friday, May12

What with unpackin the wagon an settlin everythin in our rooms an writin in my journal, it was real late by the time I turned in last night, so I kinda slept in this mornin. But that's probly the last time that'll happen. Pa an Matthew was up at dawn, an by the time I made it to the kitchen everyone else was busy with chores. Ma looked at me kinda funny an said "Nice of you to join us,

Levi, but you're too late for breakfast. You better find Pa an help him an Matthew with the milkin an the barn cleanin, that is if you're rested well enuff to take on that kinda work."

Well Ma don't usually talk to me like that less she's got her dander up so I knew better'n to make excuses. I just said "OK" an went out the door. But on the way I saw some biscuits on the counter so I snuck one.

I found Pa an Matthew just finishin up the milkin. Pa didn't say nothin bout me bein late – he probly figgered Ma had taken care a that. Then he said I had missed out on the milkin but I was just in time for the fun part a farmin -- cleanin up all the droppins.

That evenin we was all gathered in the sittin room an Ma couldn't hold it in no longer. She said to Rachel "I still can't believe you an Matthew took that long trip through New York an cross Lake Erie with a year old baby. It didn't worry me then cause I didn't know what it was like, but now I've been through it an it was awful! I don't understand how you could take that kinda chance with her."

Rachel looked kinda sideways over at Matthew, then turned back an said "We didn't have no choice, Ma. Bout a month fore we left Matthew saw two guys rob and beat a old man half to death. He tried to stop em but they knocked him around too, an then they said if he ever told anyone they'd do the same to me an the baby."

"Oh, my God!" Ma yelled. "Why didn't you ever tell us this?"

"Cause I was too scared of what them bums'd do to my family," Matthew said. "Every few days one or th'other of em would catch up with me in town at the livery or the feed store. He wouldn't say nothin but just zip two fingers cross his lips. I knew zackly what he meant. That's when me an Rachel began plannin to come west."

Then Rachel said, "I guess we was lucky. The trips on the Canal an the Lake wasn't too bad and Sarah Jane did real well. The worst part was gettin up here from Detroit. Matthew bought his first two oxen there an they was good at sloggin through the mud but they was the slowest thing God ever made. That wagon ride like to near kill us all!"

Saturday May 13

Rachel's even more into cleanin up than Ma if that's possible. She says in her house everyone gets a bath an their clothes washed every Saturday. An, as dumb as it sounds, that's what we did! They started in right after dinner time with the laundry an it took up most a the afternoon. I guess it made sense for the women's dresses cause their long skirts was always draggin in the dirt. But they washed everythin else women wear too. I left then – I didn't wanna see no part a that! But later when they tried to get me an Pa to give em our shirts an pants an all the rest, he put up a big fuss. "They's hardly even broke in from the last washin an starchin," he complained. Feelin pretty brave, I said,"Yeah!"

We expected Matthew to join us, but he musta been trained from day one – he gave in easy. Ma didn't say nothin but gave me an Pa the look that meant she weren't foolin around. So we went in the bedroom, took everythin off an handed it out the door.

Then came bath time. Back home it was one tub a hot water, men first, then the women, then the kids. But at Rachel's it's her house, her rules. Here it's two tubs, one for men, one for women – *youngest* first. Well, I don't think Pa'd ever got into a tub after someone else had used it since he was a kid. He put up such a squawk, Rachel finally agreed to put in fresh water. But I gotta give him credit. After, he swallowed his pride an thanked her.

Supper was a little late today but I gotta admit -- everyone sure looked an smelled a lot better.

Sunday, May 14

Parently the folks in Groveland is pretty religious – specially the Quakers. Back home, Rebecca was always more of a church goer than me or Sarah so she fell right into it out here. An that's why we all ended up in church this mornin. Don't know why it's called a Yearly Meetin cause they do it every month. There weren't that much to it. A buncha people sat around lookin at each other – meditatin I guess they call it -- til one of em decided to read somethin from the Bible, then the rest talked bout it. Then more sittin an lookin an readin an talkin -- they did that five or six times.

One a the readins was bout how the Jews was captured an taken to Egypt where they was treated like slaves. A couple people talked bout it, then someone asked if anyone else had somethin to say. We was all surprised when Pa got up an told bout meetin Seymour Finney in Detroit an how he was helpin slaves escape on the Underground Railroad. That started another round of talkin until a older guy stood up an told everyone to say goodbye an we all went home.

But that weren't the biggest surprise. The Russells was at the church too, Josiah, Betsey an William, an the older son Amos with his wife Esther an their kids. After all the hello's Betsey said, "It's their 10th anniversary so they thought comin down here from Flint for the weekend an goin to a prayer meetin would be a nice way to celebrate it. So we rode up last night to join em."

Ma an Betsey got to talkin with Esther an her kids while Pa, Josiah an Amos jawed bout farmin. Sarah an William moseyed off by theirselves, an I wondered if sparks mighta been flyin again.

Thursday, June 1, two weeks later

I weren't too surprised this mornin when William showed up at the door. I been kinda spectin him since we saw his family at church last month. Said he was on his way to Flint where he had some business with his brother Amos.

We chatted a few minutes bout farmin an the weather but I knew that were just polite talk. Then he asked me kinda offhand if Sarah was round. I 'lowed as how I could probly find her if he wanted to wait in the parlor.

I knew Sarah was standin at the bedroom door listenin to every word, but I took my time wanderin round lookin for her. Finally I "found" her an said, loud enuff for him to hear, "Oh, there you are. William Russell's in the parlor an asked if you was free." After a minute or two she moseyed out an said hello. Then I left the house to give em the privacy I knew they wanted.

William's business in Flint couldn't a been too urgent cause he didn't leave for more'n a hour, an afterward Sarah looked kinda flushed an couldn't stop smilin.

Tuesday, June 13

We been here bout a month now. There weren't that much to write about – just farmin chores an family stuff – 'til today. This mornin Matthew came back from the post office with a letter for Sarah. It had Jacob's return address on the outside an Sarah got so nervous she could hardly open it. She went off to the parlor to read it an bout five minutes later came back lookin like she mighta been cryin.

"What's wrong, Sarah, was it bad news?" I asked.

She said, "I don't know, Levi. I'm all kinda mixed up right now." Then she handed me the letter an went outside. Soon's I started readin I knew why she was upset.

Dear Sarah,

I don't hardly know where to begin 'cept to say I owe you a debt so deep I can never repay it.

I'm engaged to get married to Becky Wagner, a girl I've known since high school back home. We was thinkin bout it last year fore I got trampled by that horse. But when I found out that my legs would never be the same again I started pullin away from her. I knew I couldn't provide for her an a family like I should an I figgered sooner or later she'd stop lovin a guy in my condition. She tried to bring me round but I had my mind made up. When my family left New York I thought that would be the end of it and she'd find another guy.

Then I met you, Sarah, an I learned somethin on that steamboat I never thought was possible. You showed me that I can be loved by a woman even tho I'm not a whole man. Then later when I got this job in my uncle's machine shop an started to earn a decent wage, I knew I could support a family. I was plannin to write you and see if we could meet again.

Then last month I saw Becky at the State Fair in Detroit. Her family had moved here in April. We got to talkin an the old feelins started up all over. I told her bout you an how we felt bout each other then, but the more we talked the more I realized it was her I really wanted. We saw each other a lot last month an yesterday we decided to get engaged.

It's thanks to you, Sarah, that I can do this. I can't tell you how sorry I am if I've hurt you. You're a wonderful person, an I hope you find your true love as I have.

All my best wishes for you,
Jacob

The Preparation

Monday, June 26

There was a meetin of local farmers in Groveland this evenin an Matthew invited me an Pa to go along. There was lotsa talk bout last year's harvest an the crops they'd planted this spring. Some a the dairy farmers said they was worried that the bulls weren't doin their jobs cause the cows ain't birthin as many calves as they usta.

Then a tall man with lotsa black hair an a beard stood up an asked "Is anyone here planning to head to the southwest part of the state this year?" Three men raised their hands and said yes. Pa was one of em.

"Well, you better think twice about that. The ague fever's really ragaing out there. A friend of mine from Kalamazoo came through here yesterday an said a lot of folks are getting sick out there – one even died from it."

Then Doc Halberson stood up an said "Tom's right. I heard the same thing. They're calling it ague but it's really a kind of malaria. Mosquitoes brought it up from the south last year. I even had two patients from Groveland with a mild case last month. Quinine still works but it's gotten real expensive. Seems the worst is because of all the rain they had around Kalamazoo. It was so wet out there this spring they bred like wildfire. Anyone wants to go out that way should stay away from that part of the state."

After the meetin broke up Matthew introduced me an Pa to Tom Stocking, the tall guy who spoke. Pa asked him had he been out there lately.

"I haven't been where the fever is so bad Charles, but last month I went to the Ionia land office. They're handling the Goverment grants for all the land around there and I was planning to buy a couple hundred acres north of Kalamazoo. You can buy it for only $1.25 an acre. If you're not afraid of hard work there is a lot of fertile land once you get the trees cleared off. But while I was there I heard about the fever, so I started checking on lots further up, north of Grand Rapids. You planning to settle out there?"

"Yes, I was thinkin bout packin up the family an leavin next week, but my son-in-law can't seem to find a decent hand for his farm so we been helpin out. Also, his wife is spectin nother baby in the spring, an my wife would like to stay here for that. Mebbe I'll leave the family here an go out to Ionia myself just to see what they got."

"That's smart, Charles. You don't want to take your family out there without having the land you want and a cabin or some kind of shelter on the property. I'm going back the first week in July with Erastus Higbee, an old friend of mine. He's got two lots in Orleans – about 160 acres -- and he wants to start his cabin. I'm going to purchase three or four lots but still haven't decided just where. You're welcome to come with us if you want."

"That might work, Tom. Let me talk it over with the family an let you know. If I go would it be alright if Levi comes along too?"

"We welcome anyone with a good axe and muscles, an Levi looks like he's got the muscles."

I was standin next to Pa, an when I heard that it hit me – after all our travellin on the Canal an on Lake Erie an then up from Detroit, an everythin that happened along the way, we's really goin west!

This evenin Ma an Pa talked it over an she agreed. Goin to Ionia with Tom Stocking an Erastus Higbee to scout the place out was a good idea. Better to go with folks who have been there and know their way round an can help Pa pick out good land.

The next day Pa an Matthew was rubbin down the horses an Pa said, "You know, Matthew, Mike an Maggie are two of the finest horses I ever had. But if I find the kinda land I want out west they ain't gonna be much help clearin timber an plowin fields. I'm gonna need a team of oxen. With your farm cleared an planted now, you probly got more oxen than you need. How about if I trade you even these horses for two of em? "

"That hardly seems fair, Pa. Them is really fine horses. Even one a them is worth more'n two oxen. Sides, I can tell you ain't never settled in the wild. Oxen only move one or two miles in a hour. They's fine for clearin an plowin but when you want to go somewhere for supplies or mebbe come back here to visit, its horses you'll need. Take two of my oxen but keep Mike an Maggie with you too. You're gonna.need em a lot more'n me."

Pa said "Well you're probly right, Matthew, that's mighty kind of you. You're makin this easier for us in more ways'n one. Thanks for bein such a good son-in-law."

Wednesday, July 5

Yesterday was more'n the 4th a July to the people round here. They was also celebratin Michigan's first year as a state. Seems like every kid in Groveland was settin off fire crackers an rockets. I dunno where they got all them fireworks but last night sure was loud.

Next week we leave for Ionia, so today me an Pa met with Tom an Erastus to settle our plans. Course I just listened but it made me feel real good just to be there. Mostly they talked bout food an tools an what animals to take. In the end they decided on two oxen an four horses. Tom said he could bring his two draft horses, Josie an Herman. Pa figgered since the others was kinda actin like guides for him he owed em somethin, so he offered to bring the oxen an Mike an Maggie.

Then Tom said, "But it would be best if one of you knows how to drive oxen because I've never done it." Erastus said "I been drivin oxen since I was a kid, so on the way out there I'll teach you an Levi cause it's somethin you'll wanta know sooner or later."

The plan was for Pa an Tom to stop in Ionia to pick out the property they wanted an settle the deeds. Erastus would take the oxen an go on to Orleans an start clearin his land. Then we'd go help him with clearin an cuttin lumber for the cabin. While Erastus roughed out his cabin the three of us would take the oxen an start the clearin on either Pa or Tom's land, dependin on where they ended up buyin.

Thursday, July 6

This mornin Pa took the Kentucky outta the wagon an said "Levi, it's time you learned to shoot this rifle proper. Where we're goin you're gonna need it." That surprised me a bit. Peter was the only one Pa ever let use the Kentucky an he was almost as good a shot as Pa.

Pa said "There's an open field out beyond the barn with a hill at the end. We can shoot safe out there. Pick up some a them pine cones from where the trees dropped em." Then we went out to the field an put em in different places, near an far, on the ground an on the hillside.

I already knew how to load the rifle from watchin Pa an Peter, an then Mr DeGroot on the boat, so I did that without much help. Then he said "The first thing you gotta learn is how to hold it. If you ain't holdin a gun right you ain't gonna hit a thing. Which is your best eye?"

"I guess my right eye sees some better'n the left one."

"Then close your left eye an put the butt end snug up to your right shoulder. This gun's got a mighty kick, so be sure you keep that stock tight. Now grip the barrel piece an put your finger on the trigger firm but don't squeeze yet."

I was s'prised how long the Kentucky is – probly over five feet. The end kept weavin up an down. Pa said "Put your left elbow straight down under the barrel; that'll help to keep it steady." He was right bout that.

"Now the next thing you gotta learn is how to aim it. They's two sights. Look through the back one an put the front one on the target. Start with the closest pine cone – the one bout 50 yards away."

I did what he said but the front sight was still wandrin round the cone I was aimin at. Then Pa said "Take in a deep breath, let it half out – then stop an hold it while you aim an shoot." That helped keep the sight on target, but I let the rifle butt slip a bit off my shoulder a bit. When I squeezed the trigger, I thought I'd been hit with a sledge hammer. If we'd been huntin my yell woulda scared off all the game within a mile.

Pa said "Best way to member the right way to do sumthin is to do it wrong the first time. Now you won't forget to keep the butt tight on your shoulder. The reason your shot was short is called 'the drop.' Bullets don't fly in a straight line cause a gravity. You gotta aim a little above the target. Depends on how far the target is, but after lotsa practice you'll get a feel for how much."

Well, I wasn't bout to do lotsa practicin with that sore shoulder, so I figgered to try usin the left side. It felt kinda awkward at first but after a while I got to where I could hit the closest cones pretty regular. Then every few loads Pa had me shoot further out an by dinner time I was hittin some a the cones on the hillside. It was over 100 yards away.

Pa said "Levi, I b'lieve you're a natural-born shooter -- an you ain't even usin your best eye! But we're outta powder an gotta quit now. We'll get more in town cause I want you to practice a little every day. An I want you to do it on both left an right sides. That way you can be quick no matter what side your target is on."

I was glad to quit – by now both my shoulders was hurtin an I needed to rest em. But also I was real proud that Pa was teachin me to shoot his rifle.

Friday, July 7

I wonder if Ruth Ann fergot bout me. Mebbe she met nother guy while she was stayin at her uncle's fancy place on Lake Erie. It's been two months an I ain't heard a word from her. Next week we's goin off into some pretty wild country an it'll be a long time fore we get back.

This mornin me an Pa rode Mike an Maggie down to Pontiac for powder, more rope, a spare axe and some other stuff. While Pa was gettin them things I went to the Post Office for the mail. There was a letter for Rachel an some feed catalogs for Matthew. An stuck in the middle of all that was a envelope with Matthew's address on it. But the return address was R. A. Just, Lansing Township, and down in one corner was a note "Personal for Levi Broas". I nearly dropped everythin else tryin to open it, but then Pa came in an said "Let's go, Levi, it's gettin on to dinner time an Ma don't wait round for stragglers." So I shoved it in my pocket an near went crazy wonderin what it said.

When we got back dinner was on the table so I had to sit down an eat. I ate real fast but it seemed like everybody else was draggin it out, an Ma don't let nobody leave the table til we're all done. Finally, I scused myself, took a candle an a match from the cupboard, an went to the outhouse where I could read the letter in private. I read real slow to make it last.

Dear Levi,   *Saturday, July 1, 1837*

I'm sorry I took so long writing to you but we just got here yesterday. Right now we're staying in a place called Lansing Township. Before we left Detroit Papa went to the Government land office and bought three hundred acres in the Lansing Territory. He's planning to start a small dairy farm if he can get cows at a decent price.

We left Buffalo in kind of a hurry. When Papa went to repay the loan the two men from the Canal boat who tried to rob us were there. They were telling Mr. Braddock that when they tried to collect his money they were beat up and thrown in the water by some ruffians. They wanted him to pay their fee anyway. But when Papa told him what really happened, and what you and your family did to help us, Mr. Braddock said they should get out of his office and not come back.

That didn't go too well with them. As they left the one with all the tattoos said, "You cost us a lotta money Mr Smart guy but we'll get it back somehow." Well, Papa didn't wait around to find out what "somehow" meant. We said goodbye to his cousin's family the next day, packed everything and went straight to the docks.

A steamship called Michigan was just about to leave when we got there but they waited for us. During the trip to Detroit Papa got friendly with the Captain and was telling him about our trip on the Erie Canal. When he got to the part about those two thieves the Captain said he'd heard something like that a while back from another man. He figured then that it was just a made-up river tale, but now knew it must have really happened.

Papa asked him the name of the other man and he said he couldn't be sure but thought it sounded something like "Ross." Then they knew it must have been your Pa. When he came down to our cabin and told me what he'd heard I felt a chill run down my spine. It was like an omen – we're meant to be together, Levi!

There's a post office here so please write to me as soon as you know where you're family is going to settle.

Love,
Ruth Ann

I read it again, then again, specially them last three words. Soon's my heart got back where it belongs, I went in the house. Course by then everyone had figgered out who the letter was from an I got lotsa questions an teasin. I wrote her a long answer bout our trip from Buffalo to Detroit an then to Groveland. I told Ruth Ann that me an Pa was gonna leave for Ionia next week to pick out property an mebbe we could meet up along the way. Matthew said he'd mail my letter tomorrow from Pontiac cause I'm not goin to be near a post office anytime soon.

To Ionia

Monday, July 10

This mornin I got the same feelin as the day we left home in New York – kinda scared but excited too. Matthew an Rachel, Ma, Sarah, little Sarah Jane, three chickens an a cow were all in the yard sayin goodbye when we took off just after sunrise. Pa an Tom Stocking led with Mike an Maggie pullin the first wagon. Josie was tied behind. Then it was Erastus Higbee an me with the two oxen pullin the supply wagon an Herman in back. We'd decided earlier that Pa an Tom would keep on goin ahead but stop every hour an wait for us to catch up. That way they could scout for trouble with the trail or with Indians.

Tom an Erastus had been to Ionia afore, but they used different routes. Tom went north to Flint, then south on the Shiawassee Trail to the Grand River Trail. Erastus went straight west from Groveland to the Shiawassee. It was shorter but he said it was rough goin – heavy forest, bad trails and swarms of mosquitoes. So we took Tom's route.

Now let me tell you, drivin oxen is sure different from drivin horses. It's done more with voice commands than reins an that means yellin at em. They's slow an stubborn an they smell awful. I got the hang of it but it took most of a hour to go bout two miles.

The road to Flint weren't too bad, but soon's we turned south onto the Shiawassee it got worse. Steada planks there was mud an tree roots. It didn't seem to bother Mike or Maggie or the oxen too bad but Josie got a hoof caught tween two roots. The tether from Tom's wagon jerked her forward. She lost her balance, fell an broke her leg. Well, we all knew what that meant. There weren't no way that poor crippled horse could survive, even if we could bring her with us, which we sure couldn't. So Tom picked up his Kentucky an walked over to Josie. She was whinnyin somethin awful so he sat down an petted her head real gentle an spoke softly to her til she quieted. Then he stood up quick, fired, an turned away so we couldn't see his face.

That pretty much ruined the whole day. We buried Josie as best we could an then Pa an Tom decided to make camp nearby.

Thursday, July 13

Yesterday we found a trail goin west but I don't know if it had name, so I'll just call it West Trail. It weren't in a deep forest so the travelin was easier an we got to the Grand River Trail by late afternoon. Pa an Tom found a clearin near a stream so by the time me an Erastus got there they had set up camp an was cookin supper.

That evenin Tom talked bout Josie an what a good horse she was easygoin an a hard worker. But he 'lowed bout how they was gonna have to replace her. Then Erastus spoke up an said, "Mebbe we should get a mule, Tom. They're stronger, they can work longer an harder than a horse an they'll eat almost anythin."

Then Pa said, "I got a friend who was in the army when they was settlin the west and fightin Indians just bout every day. He says mules was bout all the soldiers used – for haulin, plowin an saddle ridin." Well, that kinda settled it. Tom said it might be easier than havin a horse that reminded him of Josie every time he looked at it. So they agreed to find a mule when we get to Lansing Township.

Indians

Friday, July 14

Well today didn't start out too good. Just after dawn I was still half asleep when I heard what sounded like some people talkin real soft, but I couldn't understand what they was sayin. It was like a foreign language. I sat up but nobody else was stirrin. I guess their hearin ain't as good as mine. I rolled over real quiet and poked Erastus, whisperin in his ear that I thought someone was outside the camp. He listened a bit then said to me "Them's Indians –sounds like Potawatomie. Be quiet but tell your Pa an Tom to pick up their rifles."

Tom was on th'other side a me so I woke him up first, but I'da had to crawl around him to get to Pa. By now three Indians was whoopin an runnin an shootin arrows. They was landin all around us an one grazed the side a my leg. It hurt like the dickens but there weren't no time to worry bout it. I grabbed Pa's Kentucky an me an Tom both fired. Two of em fell right away, but the third one turned an ran back toward a buncha five or six more at the other end a the clearin. By then Pa was up an I gave him the rifle. Cool as could be, he brought down another one at bout two hundred yards. When the rest a them saw that they all scooted back into the forest.

After everyone started breathin again, Erastus spoke up first. "If it weren't for Levi's good ears we mighta all got a Potawatomi haircut. Tom, I think his leg wound is just a scratch but you got some medicine trainin – you should take a look at it. Then we better get outta here fore they come back with the whole tribe. Some a them got rifles -- we're just lucky these renegades didn't."

Tom did what he could to clean an bandage my leg but he said some a the Indian tribes round here smear their arrow heads with the juice from the Yew berry. It's poison an can make the wound get real ugly. We packed up quick an got back on the trail.

The Lost Days

Monday, July 17

Mosta what I'm writin now is what others told me bout the last two days. I been in an outta things since Saturday.

I didn't sleep much Friday night cause my leg hurt so bad an I was burnin up. When Tom took the bandage off Saturday mornin it looked red and swollen. He said it was infected bad an the arrow head was either dirty or had some a that berry juice on it. He thought we could make Lansing today an we might find a doctor there.

So me an Pa took the first wagon an he pushed Mike an Maggie pretty hard, not waitin for Tom an Erastus with the oxen. I was passin out, then comin to, so Pa had me lie inside the wagon. It was a rough ride an every bump made the leg hurt worse. We hit the town just fore supper time an Pa went in the first store he saw. There was three or four old guys sittin round a cracker barrel tellin stories. One of em heard Pa tell the owner why he needed to find a doctor real quick. He stood up an said "I'm Dr Hans Friedrich, the town veterinarian. Doc Jorgenson is the people doctor. He's out of town right now but should be back in a day or two. I treat every kind of flesh wound, man or beast, so bring the boy in here and I'll take a look at him."

Pa said "I don't think he can walk. Can you come out to the wagon?"

He did an when he took off the bandage the vet said "Wow! How did he do this?"

Pa told him what happened an what Tom said bout the arrow bein dirty or mebbe havin some kinda berry juice on the tip.

"Well, from the looks of this, I'd say it was the berry juice. My farm is just down the road. Come with me and I'll clean it and put on a bread and milk poultice. That should start drawing out the poison, but you'll have to replace it every few hours. Are you going to be in town for a while? I think you should see Doc J. soon as he gets back."

Pa answered "We wasn't plannin to stay but we gotta get this cured."

At his farm he had a hospital for large animals. Pa told me later the vet spent almost a hour fiddlin with my leg an puttin that poultice stuff on. Then he helped me drink water with some powder made from willow bark. He said to Pa "That should help cut the pain. It's a bad infection, so come by here tomorrow – I want to take another look at him."

But when I tried to get up the whole room went round in circles an I hit the floor -- hard. Then the vet said "Mr. Broas, it looks like your son is too sick to go anywhere. He better stay here tonight so I can keep an eye on him."

Pa took the Doc aside an asked "How bad is it – really?"

"Well, Yew berry poisoning can be very serious. His chances depend on how strong his heart is. But at his young age it's probably very good and his body should be able to fight the poison. If there was a hospital nearby that's where I'd put him, but there isn't and he's in no shape to travel to Grand Rapids. So with Doc Jorgenson gone, leaving him with me is the best thing you can do."

"My wife an I already lost one son, Doc, an it was real hard on her. If we was to lose Levi, I think she'd go plumb outta her mind."

So they took me into the farm house. Their oldest son said he'd sleep in the barn so I could have a bed where Doc an Mrs Friedrich could look after me durin the night. An I guess it was a busy night. They told me later I was delerius or somethin like that. I went back an forth tween sleepin an yellin. Mrs F changed the poultice an tried to cool me with a ice pack. Doc said the pain was partly from the poultice drawin out the infection. That must be what they mean when they say the cure is worse than the ill.

Anyway, somethin musta worked cause by mornin I weren't so hot and my leg didn't hurt as much. Mrs F kept changin the poultice an givin me that willow powder stuff. Mebbe that's why I spent most a Sunday tryin to remember what happened to Saturday. Last night I slept a lot better, an when I woke up this mornin I felt pretty good. The fever was gone an the wound weren't so red.

Doc Jorgenson was back in town and came out to the vet farm. After lookin me over he said he knew when he left that Doc an Mrs Friedrich was a good backup team for him, an that Hans could be a people doctor if he wanted. Then he said my leg is healin well and I should start movin round, but not try to travel for a couple more days.

By Saturday evenin Tom an Erastus had caught up an stopped at the same store askin bout us. They was told where Doc Friedrich took me an Pa. When they got here Pa told em we wouldn't be movin for a while so they set up a camp nearby. But this mornin Pa told em I was lookin better an they should go on ahead. Tom agreed an said on the way he was gonna look for a livery stable that sells mules. Then he said when he gets to Ionia he would visit the land office while Erastus goes on to Orleans to start clearin his land.

While all this was goin on I was secretly thankin those Potawatomie for shootin me cause now we was gonna be stuck in Lansing a little longer. I asked Pa if mebbe we could try to find the Just family so he could say hello to Mr. J. I guess I weren't foolin him none but he smiled an said "Sure, Levi, we can try but I don't know where to start. All we have now is a post office address an that don't tell us where they're boardin."

But Tom heard us talkin an said "There's a land office in Lansing that should have a record of Mr. J's purchase. He's probably out there now working on the land. If they'll tell us where it is

Erastus and I could stop on our way out and tell him you're here but can't travel right now."

Then I said "Thanks Tom, that'd mighty nice. But you gotta know, the last time I saw Ruth Ann her Papa weren't too happy bout us bein together. He may not want her to know we're here."

"Well, at least we can try, Levi."

Ruth Ann

Tuesday, July 18

I spent this mornin doin nuthin an it was pretty borin. After dinner Pa said "Levi, you better get some exercise. Let's take a short walk out to the barn an back." It felt good at first but by the time we got back to the porch I was plumb wore out. I near collapsed into a chair an fell hard asleep. As usual, I was dreamin bout Ruth Ann. We was back on the Canal boat again, goin through the locks at Rochester. She musta come up from behind me cause I smelled her fore I saw her – it was like a buncha lilacs. But then I was wakin up an the smell was still there. My heart started pumpin faster fore I even opened my eyes, an there she was standin in front a me. I was tryin my darndest to get outta the chair when Ruth Ann reached out, took my hand an helped me up. She said "Hello Levi. How are you feeling?" After I got over the shock I said "Hi Ruth Ann. A lot better now." Another one a my big speeches.

In the yard there was a horse an buggy an Mr an Mrs Just was gettin down from it. They came up on the porch an Mr J turned to me an said "Your friends found us and told us about your encounter with the Indians. That must have been quite a scary time."

"Actually, Mr. Just, we was so busy fightin we didn't have time to be scared."

Then Mrs J took my hand. She said "Levi, the Lord must have been watching over you. You were really fortunate to find such a good doctor."

"He's a vet, Mrs. Just, the only doctor in town right then. Doc Friedrich said if he hadn't got that wound treated when he did the arrow poison woulda killed me in a few more hours. Then him an Mrs Friedrich nursed me for two more days like I was their own son."

"Well, you're here now and we're so glad you pulled through that awful ordeal."

Ruth Ann looked at me then an said "Feel up to taking a walk?"

All of a sudden I felt like I coulda run a marathon. With a chance to get off by ourselves, I said "Sure."

On the way she said "Levi, when Papa made us stay in Buffalo and you left on the boat I was afraid he was trying to keep us apart and I'd never see you again. Then at his cousin's home on Lake Erie there were always parties and games with lots of people around. At first it was fun, but after a while they all seemed kinda phony, the girls talking about their fancy homes and clothes, and the boys flirting and making suggestive comments. All I could think about was how different you are from them and how much I wanted to be with you instead."

I knew then that it was time for another speech, but this time I was ready. "Ruth Ann, you don't know how much I wanted to hear you say that. Cept for Indians an fever, you're bout the only thing I've thought of for more'n two months." Then I told her all bout the storm on Lake Erie, our travels through the forest, Josie breakin her leg, the Indian attack an all the care I got from the Friedrichs.

I asker her "But Ruth Ann, there's somethin I don't understand. When we left Buffalo I thought your Papa didn't want us to be together any more. But here he was drivin you to see me."

"That's kind of a long story, Levi. When your friends Tom and Erastus found us I was helping Papa clear trees and brush from the land he bought. When they told us you were in Lansing I about jumped out of my skin, but Papa didn't look too happy. Then they said you'd been hurt by Indians and were fighting to stay alive. I felt a lump in my throat I couldn't swallow, and I said "'Papa, I've got to see Levi. If you won't take me there I'll walk!'

"Well, he knew I meant it. Besides, he still feels a debt to your family for your help on the Canal boat. We went back to the lodge where we're staying and told Mama what had happened. She insisted on coming along, so we all got in the buggy and came here."

By now we was alongside the barn an I decided there'd been enough talkin. I pulled her close an kissed her, long an slow. It was only our second kiss an it felt so good – there weren't no hurt this time.

Ionia

Thursday, July 20

This mornin Doc Friedrich said I was well enough to start our trip again. Fore we left Pa said "Doctor an Mrs Friedrich, we can't thank you folks enuff for the way you treated us. You saved my son's life an for that I can never repay you. But can't I give you somethin for your time and care?"

"That's ok, Charles. Seeing Levi pull through that ordeal is reward enough. Besides, we only charge for treating creatures with *four* legs."

So we said goodbye to them, hitched up Mike an Maggie to the wagon an got back on the trail. But fore leavin Lansing I talked Pa into stoppin at the lodge where the Justs was stayin. While he was talkin with Mr an Mrs J, me an Ruth Ann stepped outside for one last kiss. That made three, an yes, I was countin!

Fore we left I shook Mr. J's hand an said "Thanks for comin to see me at the vet's. That really helped." He said "Sure," but his handshake was kinda limp. Then Mrs. J gave me a big hug an whispered in my ear "Come see us any time, Levi."

The trail weren't too bad as far as Portland so we got there fore dinner an made camp. But right after eatin it started in to rain so I'm tryin to keep dry while writin this

Friday, July 21

It rained all night so everythin west a Portland was real muddy all the way to Ionia. The air was hot an sticky an there was a lotta puddles. Mosquitoes love that as much as they love people, so we did a lot of slappin an cussin til Pa membered somethin Ma had packed for us. He dug in one a the packs an found her can a fennel paste. We smeared it all over the bare parts an it helped, I guess cause the bugs probly hated that smell as much as we did.

To get to Ionia we had to cross the Grand River. It were way too big to ford, specially after all the rain. Pa drove downstream coupla miles fore he found a boy bout my age sleepin next to a ferry boat crossin. I woke him up kinda easy so's not to scare him an asked when the next boat's due in. He said "It's bout halfway cross on the way to Ionia. Should be back in twenty, thirty minutes. Cost for two horses an wagon is two dollars. You can pay me now – save time when the boat gets here. "

I guess I woulda done it but Pa weren't born yesterday. He said "Thanks anyways, but we'll wait for the boat captain."

By the time the ferry docked bout a half hour later the boy had disappeared. When Pa asked the boat skipper the fare for a wagon an two horses, he said "On weekdays just a dollar, but it's gotta be hard coin. I don't take no paper money." Pa paid him an then told him bout the boy askin two dollars. "That thievin kid hangs round here most everytime I go cross, but he's always gone by time I come back. If I ever catch up with him I'm gonna load his britches with buckshot!"

Mike an Maggie didn't take too kindly to the ferry boat ride – they started whinnyin an buckin soon's we took off. But Pa's got a way with horses. He petted em an talked real gentle, an they quieted right down. I thought the boat ride was great. It was the first time I'd gone anywhere in Michigan without gettin bumped an bounced around.

Time we docked it was gettin on to dusk so we made camp next to the river.

Saturday, July 22

Yesterday the skipper had told Pa where the Ionia land office is so first thing this mornin that's where we headed. Pa asked the goverment man if Tom Stocking had shown up, an when we told him our names he said "Mr Stocking told me you'd be coming by here soon. He bought several parcels in Sections 14 and 15. Look at that map on the wall and you can see they're on both sides of the Flat River."

Then he said "there's still some good land north of his. How much are you looking to buy?"

"I think bout 300 acres, an I want it to border the east side a the Flat."

"We have some choice property available up there in Sections 10 and 11. Here, let me show you on the map. If you put these four lots together you'll have 320 acres and it's almost surrounded by this loop in the river."

"That looks like just what I want. How much'll it cost?" Pa knew the answer to that but he was testin the man.

"All this land is going for $1.25 an acre, so that comes to an even $400." So Pa signed some papers an paid the man. Good thing they took paper money! Then Pa asked him "How do we know when we get to our land? It's nothin but trees an swamp round here."

"First of all, I'll give you the deed and a description of your purchase, as well as a map of the area with your lots marked on it. There's also a copy of the surveyor's field notes that describe the corner posts and the witness trees marking your property. There's a trail going northwest from here. Take that until you come to the Flat River, then just follow it north until you hit the first of Mr Stocking's marking stakes. Your lots are the ones just north of his."

Pa thanked the man, stuffed all the papers an the receipt in his carry sack an we left the office. It's a good thing this day is done an we can get back to the camp. I'm ready to collapse. Guess I'm not as healed as I thought.

Erastus's Land

Sunday, July 23

Soon's we got up this mornin Pa said "How you feelin now, Levi?"

"Lot better'n last night, I reckon, Pa. Guess I really needed to sleep."

"Well, that's good cause today we gotta find Tom an Erastus. Tom coulda gone on to his property or they might both be in Orleans on Erastus's land. That's closer so stead a goin over to the Flat like the man said we'll go there first."

The trail from Ionia to Orleans weren't much bigger'n a coupla footpaths. We pushed our way through, but tree branches kept slappin at us an scrapin the sides a the wagon. The land office man had given us the number an location of Erastus property, but with all them trees every lot looked like every other lot. Pa kept watchin for corner posts an when he found one he started callin out for Erastus an Tom. Pretty soon there was answerin hoots an then there they was, cuttin timber round a small clearin.

Tom came over to me an said "Glad you're better, Levi. When Erastus and I left Lansing I wasn't sure I'd ever see you again."

"Yeah, I was pretty sick. But that vet and his wife worked hard to keep me on this side a the grass. I ain't never gonna forget them two." Erastus didn't say nothin but he grabbed my hand an just held on.

Pa told Tom where the land was he'd bought, an they agreed we'd go to Tom's place first since it was on the way. But for a coupla days we was gonna help Erastus cut an trim some more trees. Then we'll go north an look over our properties.

Tom said to me an Pa "Come on over here – I want you to meet Jenny, the newest member of our team." She was gray, smaller than Mike or Maggie an had a mean look on her face. When I went to pet her she reared her head round an tried to nip my arm.

Tom said "Some mules are like that, Levi. They don't want to be touched. And whatever you do, don't stand behind her. She may be small but she's got a vicious kick." I had already decided to give Jenny a lotta room.

Me an Tom started cuttin an trimmin while Pa an Erastus was settin logs for the base of the cabin. I been swingin a axe ever since I was taller'n one, an I tried to keep up, but after bout a hour I was plumb tuckered out. Tom told me to rest a while an then if I felt like it I could cook some sausages for supper.

Tom's Land

Wednesday, July 26

By the time we left him this mornin Erastus had a pretty good start on his cabin, an enough timber cut to finish it. He thought we should take the ox team an just leave him Jenny an a wagon. Tom said he should have Herman too so he could ride into Ionia. But Erastus said he'd be fine without a horse cause he'd rather ride Jenny.

Then Tom said "OK, Levi, you can drive the oxen. Your Pa and I'll ride in the wagon. We'll let Herman, Mike and Maggie trail behind – they've earned a rest. But give their tethers lotsa slack. We don't want any of them to fall ..... like Josie did." He had trouble gettin that last part out.

This time we headed over to the Flat River, meanin to follow it to Tom's property. That stream sure was a pretty sight -- tumblin an splashin an curvin every hundred yards or so. It looked like God couldn't make up His mind what to do with it. I figgered there must be lotsa fish in it, mebbe even better'n the Bradley back home.

With the three of us watchin for corner posts we found Tom's lots easy. Up here the river got wider so it was pretty smooth, an that was good cause his property was on both sides of it.

Tom said he weren't ready to build a cabin yet – probly not til next year -- but he wanted to make sure anyone knew the land was his. We found a small clearin bout 10 yards across an set out to make it bigger an put up a crude hut. An that's when I got to see them oxen earn their keep. Pa an Tom did the choppin while I hooked them beasts to the drag hook an towed the timber to the center of the clearin. To them, it was like they was pullin toothpicks. I ain't never seen such brute strength.

Tom made a sign with his name an the property numbers on it for both sides a the river an fastened it to the hut. We was done by supper time an everyone thought it was a good day's work.

Abraham Roosa

Thursday, July 27

The three of us set out bout sunrise an followed the river bank. We'd just found the southwest corner stake for Pa's property when I thought I smelled smoke. I looked north an saw a white cloud risin outta the trees longside the river. We got off the wagon an Pa laid the Kentucky cross the crook in his elbow kinda lazy like an let it point at the ground. We picked our way through the woods real quiet. When we got to the clearin we saw a big, shaggy lookin fella sittin next to a camp fire. His clothes was ragged an his hair hung in bunches down to his shoulders. An what he was cookin smelled worse'n the oxen.

Pa walked up behind the man an asked "You really plan on eatin that, friend?" The man near jumped outta his skin. He started to reach for his own rifle, then turned an saw Pa's, so he changed his mind bout that. I could tell he was kinda young, but seein Pa with the gun didn't frighten him none. "Sure. It's my dinner," he said. "An what's it to ya anyways?"

Pa kinda chuckled an said "I really don't care if you wanna poison yerself, son. But I do wanna see yer copy of the deed to this property."

"This is just open goverment land mister. I don't need no deed to be here."

"Well, I gotta admit, that were true until I bought it last week. Now you're my guest, an I don't let my guests eat garbage. Stoke that fire a bit so Levi can cook us all a proper meal."

I don't know who was more surprised – me or the stranger. We just kinda stared at each other while Pa an Tom set about feedin an waterin the animals. Finally, I said "I'm Levi, case you hadn't figgered that out. Who are you an what brought you here?"

"My name is Abraham Roosa. I'm on my way to Ionia to find a job. I didn't see no markins showin this was anyone's property. I'm all outta ammo an I ain't et in two days. When I saw that dead gopher I figgered to cook it an eat it right here fore I pass out." Then he stopped and looked real puzzled. "Is your Pa really gonna feed me?"

"Pa don't never say things twice. If that's what he said that's what he meant. 'Sides, it's what people do out here in the woods."

"Well I'll be damned. Nobody's ever treated me like that. Is there somethin I can do to pay you back?"

"Yeah, first you can bury that dead thing. Then chop up some more kindlin an get the fire goin again while I peel the taters. Then go help Pa an Tom with the oxen."

While we was eatin I asked him bout his name again cause I weren't sure I heard him right. When he said "Abraham Roosa," Pa looked up sudden like and said "Huh -- there's a Abraham Roosa in our family – Levi's granddaddy on his mother's side – but you sure ain't old enough to be him."

"That's kind of a long story. Sure you want to hear it?"

"Yeah, if anyone deserves to know where you come from it's us. Sides, I never heard tell of him havin a relation with his name."

"My Pa was one a Abraham Roosa's distant relations. He was carryin on with a young girl from a nearby farm an she ended up pregnant. Old man Roosa was pretty fussy bout the family name so he paid her to leave town to birth me, an to put me in a home for kids with no family. She was kimda upset bout that but she did it anyways. But when they asked her my name she said "Abraham Roosa II" an it stuck.

"I grew up there but I left when I was fifteen an wandered round New York doin farm work. I'm pretty good with a hammer an saw so I got into barn buildin for a while. Then a drought hit. Times got tough for farmers an the work kinda dried up too."

Pa asked him "How'd you get all the way out here?"

"After a few months of bummin round I got a job guidin horses on the Erie Canal. The work was OK but I got fed up real quick with the way them horses was treated. I tried to care for em when we was in dock but the company drove em so hard they didn't last more'n a year or two. When we hit Buffalo I went to the docks lookin for a job on a Lake Erie steamboat. The captain of the General Gratiot said he needed a extra deck hand so I did that for bout three years. I kinda liked bein out on the water where everythin was wide open.

"Then one day a passenger said he was plannin to travel through Michigan all the way to Grand Rapids an he needed somebody who could handle horses. By then I had been thinkin I'd like to see some a the west, so I took the job. An I was real good at it too.

"It was a long, tough trip, kinda hard on the horses. But I saw to it they was well fed an watered an I groomed an rested em every night. Turns out they was the best friends I ever had.

"But when we got to Grand Rapids the man tried to cheat me outta half my pay. So that night I snuck into his room an took what he owed me. Course then I had to disappear, an I been stickin to the woods ever since, trappin an huntin. Headed down toward Kalamazoo but kept runnin into people sick with the ague. So I got away from there real quick.

"Ran into some Ottawa along the Thornapple River, an traded some a my skins for a canoe. I rowed the Thornapple north to the Grand, then the Flat up to here. But let me tell you, goin upstream on the Flat with all its turns an twists really wore me out. I had to quit here. I was so tired an sore I didn't care whose land it was."
"So Abraham, you're tellin us you're some kinda blood relation. But how do we know it's true?"

"Well, mebbe this'll prove it. The people my Ma left me with was real religious. They told me later that I got pretty sick early on an they was afraid I wouldn't live much longer so they had me baptized in their church. When I fooled em all an pulled through they took the baptism paper an put it with my other stuff. I've been carryin that with me ever since."

He dug a crumpled up paper outta his sack an handed it to Pa who smoothed it out an studied it real good. Then he gave it to me an sure nuff, it was all official lookin:

Abraham Roosa II, baptized in the Lord
this 23rd day of June 1817.
First Congregational Church of Jesus Christ
Ulster, New York.

Pa reached over to him, shook his hand an said, "Well, I guess that settles it, Abraham. Welcome to the family!"

I said, "Yeah," but I still wasn't too sure bout this guy.

Friday, July 28

This mornin at breakfast Pa said, "I was plannin for Levi, Tom an me to build a rough shelter on the property this year, then come back next year an make it bigger an better. But Abraham, if you'd be willin to work with us I'd pay you a decent wage an we could do the whole cabin this year. Then if you want, you could stay in it this winter, keepin the Indians an poachers away. If you finish up the inside work – a window, table, shelves an the like, I'll pay you the same wage. Then next year I can bring all my family out here to live."

"Wow! I ain't never had a offer like that. Sure, fer that kinda job I'll do anythin that needs doin!"

I wondered if Pa mebbe trusted this stranger-with-a-good-story too far. Sure, he had a family name, but he was really a forest bum who stole money from his employer. But Pa's usually a good judge of people, so I didn't say nothin.

After breakfast we set about clearin timber, an once again I was real glad we had them oxen. With me drivin the team an the other three choppin, we near had the base of the cabin set fore suppertime. An that's when it happened.

Abraham was in the middle of a axe swing when he just stopped, sat down on a log an put his head tween his knees. I got offa the rig to see what was wrong but time I got there he had slid off an was layin on the ground. His face had turned kinda red an he was breathin fast. I touched his head an it was really hot.

Tom came over an felt his neck for a pulse. "His heart's still beating but it's not very strong. I think it's the ague -- it usually hits real sudden. I saw this last year when I was down near Kalamazoo where the mosquitoes are real thick, an he was there just last week. We got to get the fever down – Levi, give me the water bucket."

I handed the bucket to Tom an he slowly poured it all on Abraham's head an chest, bein careful not to get it in his nose or mouth. That brought him back from wherever he'd gone, but by now he had turned a awful gray. He was mumblin somethin bout the home an the kids he grew up with, but to me he looked like he was more dead than alive.

Pa asked Tom "What do we do now? Is he gonna make it?"

"If he's going to pull through he'll need a lot of liquids and rest for a few days. I saw about a dozen cases of ague when I was down there and only two of them died. But the others were pretty useless for most of a week."

Pa said "Levi, go fix somethin in the wagon for him to lay on, then we'll carry him over there. Tom, is there any medicine you know of that'll fight this?"

"Well, the Ottawa have a potion they say helps, but I don't know what it is. We passed one of their settlements on the way up here. I know a little of their language so maybe Levi and I should ride down there tomorrow. Abraham still has some good beaver skins. Maybe they'll trade for some of the potion.

We made supper for the three of us. I got Abraham to eat a little thin porridge but he couldn't keep it down. I'll try again tomorrow.

Saturday, July 29

Abraham had kind of a bad night. Every time he fell asleep he'd thrash around an wake up yellin. Musta been a fever dream cause he was still pretty hot. I kept givin him sips a cool water an wipin his head an chest with it. That helped for a bit til he fell asleep an woke up yellin again.

Me an Tom took off right after breakfast an got outside the Indian camp in a couple hours. Tom had said some a the Ottawa was friendly with whites, but I gotta admit, I was a little scared bout bein there after what happened tween me an the Potawatomi last month. Tom knew that so he told me to wait there. He said "I don't want to look threatining so I'll go in alone without a rifle. But you keep a sharp eye on me and the Kentucky on them." Then he picked up the skins an went into the camp.

Now I think back on it, that didn't seem too smart. A white man with no weapon walkin into the middle a people he was takin land from. An then askin em to do him a favor!

Well anyway, it worked out okay. These Ottawa was pretty friendly, an Tom must be a good talker, even in their tongue. It took a while but in bout a hour he came back with some a the potion. It was kind of a gooey liquid so I asked him if we was sposed to rub it on Abraham or have him drink it. Tom said the Chief told him that the potion's powers work best when the spirits are most active. He said to mix it with water an have him drink a swallow at sunrise facin east an another at sunset facin west.

Sounds kinda weird to me but it's worth a try. I just hope Abraham can keep it inside a him.

Sunday, July 30

Well, last night he kept the sunset dose down an even held onto some thin porridge. An the same thing again this mornin at sunrise. But that don't mean he's better. He's still awful gray an weak as a kitten. We made him as comfortable as we could an put water an light food where he could reach it, then went back to work on the cabin.

Monday, August 7, a week later

We gave Abraham that Ottawa potion just like the Chief said, every sunup an sundown. Them spirits musta been real powerful cause he's almost back to his self. First thing he did when he got over his silly jabberin (Tom called it "delerium") an could talk straight was to thank Tom for goin into that Ottawa camp alone for the potion. "That was a real brave thing to do, an I ain't gonna fergit it," he said.

He ain't up to swingin a axe yet but he can take over drivin the oxen, an that means there's three of us choppin again.

Since Pa showed me how to shoot the Kentucky I been practicin every chance I get. Fact, I'm kinda the main game hunter for keepin us fed with rabbit or beaver. But today I spotted a deer at bout a hundred yards, just grazin kinda lazy-like. I drew a bead behind his shoulder an fired an he dropped like a stone. I was glad a that cause I hate woundin any animal – it just ain't right.

After dressin the buck I brought what I could carry back to the camp. The four of us had a great dinner today an Pa salted what was left.

Goin Home

Wednesday, September 6, a month later

We spent most of a month cuttin, haulin an trimmin trees, notchin em an puttin em together to build the the walls, the roof an the floor. Then we caulked all the cracks with swamp mud cause it dries hard an slick. So now the cabin's a shelter from the weather but it's a long way from done. Finishin up the inside'll keep Abraham busy til spring. We'll leave Herman with him so he can get into Ionia for food an supplies. We'll leave the oxen too cause we won't need em back home an they's awful to travel with. Sides, Abraham might want to do some plowin an plantin come spring. Pa paid him six months in advance with the promise of a bonus next year if the inside was done satisfactory. (I still got my fingers crossed bout this guy.)

An tomorrow mornin me, Pa an Tom are fixin to start the trip back to Groveland. The leaves are turnin an the nights are gettin pretty cold. We been sleepin on the floor a the cabin but it's awful damp cause the fireplace ain't done yet. Finishin that'll likely be the first job Abraham gets to.

But it ain't goin home that's got me excited bout leavin here. It's stoppin in Lansing on the way.

Thursday, September 7

Just fore we left Lansing in July, I'd told Ruth Ann we'd probly be comin back through there sometime in September. She made me promise to write her from Ionia on the way down so she knew bout when to expect us. Now we's just travellin with Mike an Maggie an the wagon so we might get there fore a letter does. But I'll write anyway case we get held up.

Pa said he wants to stop by Erastus Higbee's place in Orleans on the way down to see if he plans to stay the winter or come back east with us. It'd be fine with me if he comes – I like Erastus –

but if he rides Jenny, that ornery plug of a mule will slow us down consid'able.

Friday, September 8

Well, Erastus had his cabin pretty well finished when we got there. He had decided to winter there an work on the inside. We told him the story bout Abraham an that he was doin pretty much the same thing. Erastus said he'd ride up there one day an see how he's doin with the work, or whether he'd took off with Pa's money. Pa laughed at that, but I thought it was a great idea.

Without Jenny to slow us down we got to Ionia by mid-afternoon. While Tom an Pa looked for a place to eat I went to the post office an asked if there was any mail for Broas or Stocking. When the postman said there was somethin for a Levi Broas I near fell over. Sure nuff it was from Ruth Ann. It was real short – she just wanted to tell me they had moved outta the lodge and was livin on their property now. She told us how to find it but Tom had already been there so he knew the way. But the way it ended was different.

See you soon -- Ruth Ann

I looked hard for the word "Love" but couldn't find it.

Lansing

Sunday, September 10

Yesterday we set up camp on the Grand River coupla miles west a Lansing. That's cause we wasn't bout to go callin on the Just's without takin baths. We even washed our clothes with some a Ma's home-made bar soap. An by time we got into town this mornin we was shiny clean an the clothes was almost dry.

As we was pullin up to the Just's place they was leavin, all dressed up. Mr J said "Good morning Charles and hello again Tom. We were expecting you later this month, We're on our way to church services and we're a bit late, but we should be back sometime after noon." Then he clucked to his horses an drove away.

Right then I knew somthin was wrong cause Mr J didn't even mention my name an Ruth Ann was lookin down into the carriage steada at me. I wanted to ask her what was wrong, but I knew that we couldn't talk bout it with her whole family round.

Well, that not only wiped out the mornin, it also turned my life upside down. I tried to figger out what was goin on or what I did that hurt Ruth Ann. Was it arrivin early? Or not writin sooner? We was nowhere near a post office for near two months, but mebbe I shoulda rode back to Ionia to mail her a letter. Or did her Pa finally convince her that we was too young to get serious? Or mostly, that I weren't good nuff for her?

My mind was goin crazy tryin to understand why she wouldn't look at me. Finally I decided I couldn't figger it out by myself. I just had wait for a chance to talk to her. So I went back to the camp with Tom an Pa.

Later that afternoon I decided I couldn't let things stew no longer. I saddled up Mike an rode to the Just's place, hopin to catch Ruth Ann by herself. When I got there I was still in the woods but near enuff to see her an a guy bout my age out fronta the cabin, talkin real earnest like. He was kinda tall an muscley lookin, with lotsa yellow, curly hair. An a course Ruth Ann was beautiful. If she was a stranger, I'da said they're a good-lookin couple, but a course she ain't no stranger. She's the girl that had just busted my heart into a lotta little pieces.

I turned round an rode back to the camp. Pa was fixin supper but I said I weren't hungry an just wanted to take a walk. He musta know'd right then that somethin was wrong cause I ain't never not humgry.

I went down to the river an sat on the bank. The water was rushin by, gurglin an jumpin over some fallen trees – made me think of the Flat River up near our property. Then I thought bout Ruth Ann an it all came out. I'm too old to cry but I did anyway – long an hard.

I guess I didn't hear him cause a the rushin water. First thing I knew Pa sat down next to me. He didn't say nothin, just sat there lookin at the river like me. After a few minutes he asked "Wanna talk bout it?"

Monday, September 11

I can't believe all that happened today. I'll start with yesterday.

Back at the river, me an Pa talked so long supper was cold by time we got to camp. I told him everythin that was botherin me bout Ruth Ann an all the things I feared might be goin on. But mostly, I said I was afraid I'd lost her.

He listened real careful but didn't say much at first. Then he turned an looked straight at me an said, "Listen to me, Levi, you're jumpin to conclusions. I understand why you're upset, but there could be lotsa other things happenin to her that you know nothin bout. You go over there tomorrow an don't leave til you've been able to talk to her an get it all out."

So that's what I did. This mornin after breakfast I rode to the Just place an knocked on the door. Mr. J answered, lookin surprised when he saw me. "Oh – uh, good morning Levi. What can I do for you?"

"I'd like to talk to Ruth Ann, Mr. Just. Is she home?"

"Can I ask what it's about, Levi?"

"It's kinda personal, sir, but I think you know what it's about."

"Yes, I think I do, and I don't believe she wants to see you right now."

Just then Ruth Ann walked round from the back of the cabin an saw me standin there. She started to turn back but I caught up to her an touched her arm. She stopped an looked down at the ground. Her Pa watched us from the door for a minute, then went back in an closed it.

At that, everythin changed. She looked up at me an I could see her eyes was kinda wet. "Let's take a walk, Levi."

We went into the woods a ways where there was some fallen trees fore she stopped an turned to me. "Sit down Levi. We've got to have a serious talk."

"That's all I been wantin to do since yesterday, Ruth Ann. When you wouldn't look at me or even say hello, an then your Papa just drove off, I kinda fell apart."

"I know, and I feel awful about that. But there's something you've got to know about my father. He was raised in a family that used fighting and violence for everything they needed or wanted. One of his brothers was even killed in a fight over the boundaries of the family farm. When Papa was finally able to get out on his own he swore he would never use a gun or even strike another person. And he vowed that violence would never be a part of his own family. He is a very serious believer in the Bible adage 'Turn the other cheek.'

"Levi, he respects your family and is really grateful for what you all did to help us out of that awful situation on the Canal boat last spring. But that also showed him how good you and your father are at fighting. And the stories about shooting Indians and killing a bear added to it. He realizes it was all done for good reasons, but he thinks those experiences are just a part of who you are and how you think when there's trouble.

"I know what a kind, gentle person you really are, but Papa says "Like father like son." He thinks you could change over time and might become like the family he grew up in. He doesn't want me to be a part of that, so he's been pushing me to see other boys."

"Is that why your father stopped in Buffalo, an why you were talkin to that yellow-haired guy yesterday?"

"Yes, his name is Kurt Johansson. He's the son of a family we met at church this summer, but it's kind of a long story.

"You see, the closest hospital is in Grand Rapids, so our pastor has set up space for a clinic in the church building. There's a Dr. O'Malley who comes there two mornings a week and another woman and I volunteer as nurses. Of course we'll go to a home anytime if there's an emergency.

"The first time we met the doctor it was apparaent that he talked with a dialect that sounded just like my Papa's, so I asked him what part of Ireland he came from. When he said Antrim County I felt a kind of warmth to meet someone from our homeland. I said, "That's where my parents are from too!" The next Sunday at church I introduced him to Papa and Mama and they've become good friends.

"Anyway, one night last August Mr. Johansson sent his other son Robert to our cabin and asked me to meet Dr. O'Malley at their home. He said Kurt was moving equipment in his father's store and cut his leg pretty bad on a plow blade. When we got there Doctor O'Malley said he wanted me to clean the wound and then assist him while he sewed it. He tried to dull the pain by rubbing a cocaine powder on the leg first, but he said it was kind of a new technique and he wanted me to comfort the patient in case that didn't work. Well, I don't know how much it helped, but Kurt kept moaning and leaning against me and holding onto my hand.

"After the doctor was finished I bandaged the wound. Then he told Kurt not to walk for a few days so the stitches could start to heal. We talked for a while and then Robert took me home.

"About a week later Kurt came over and said he wanted to thank me for my help. He gave me a small package and when I opened it there was a bracelet with a silver heart hanging from it. I looked closer and saw that it was engraved:

Ruth Ann & Kurt

"I thanked him for the thought but said I couldn't accept it because it looked so expensive. Then I added, 'But mostly, Kurt, it's because we're not a couple.'

"But he said, 'Well, not yet, Ruth Ann, but just keep it cause someday we will be.' I insisted on returning it to him but that didn't sit too well. I think he was not used to being rejected, especially by a girl. He said, 'Well, I know we're meant to be together, Ruth Ann, but if you ain't ready yet I'll keep it til you are.' And then he left.

"Since then Papa's gotten real friendly with the family an has been pushing me to see Kurt every chance he gets. When we're with our families he's a perfect gentleman. But when we're alone, he's just like the boys in Buffalo, with only one thing on his mind. That's not what I'm looking for in a date or a boyfriend. I'm sure being married to the right person must be great, but it's got to be a lot more than physical. Don't you agree, Levi?"

"I sure do, Ruth Ann. It's why you've gotten so deep into me. You're very beautiful an all that, but it's all of you that I've fallen for, inside an out." When I said that she took hold a my hand an squeezed it.

"I feel the same way about you, Levi, but Papa's set on me carrying on with Kurt. Mr. Johansson owns the general store in Lansing and sells just about everything people need, so they're pretty big in this town. Both he and Papa think Kurt and I would be a great match. But he's so possessive, and he's used to getting his own way. I've only known him a month and already he acts like I belong to him."

"I respect your Papa, Ruth Ann, an I understand why he's actin that way. He just wants what he thinks is the best for you an he's sure it ain't me. But I'm gonna prove him wrong. I don't like violence neither, but some things you just gotta fight for. Nothin's gonna stop me from seein you if it's what you want – not your Papa or Kurt what's-his-name or anyone else!"

At that she moved close an leaned in to kiss me. I took her in my arms an held on for a long time. Then I said "I've never been in love before Ruth Ann, but if this is what it feels like then I'm in it!"

She said "So am I, Levi, and now I'm gonna tell Papa and Kurt!" Then she kissed me again.

*   *   *

He musta been walkin like a hunter cause we never knew he was there. First thing we heard was this voice behind us sayin "What are you gonna tell me, Ruth Ann?"

We both jumped like scared rabbits, but fore I could even turn round Kurt grabbed me by the neck an squeezed til I couldn't breathe. I musta passed out for a few minutes cause the next thing I knew I was lyin on the ground an he was draggin Ruth Ann, screamin an kickin, over to his horse. He threw her on, then he got up behind her an rode off into the woods.

Soon's I could get up I staggered after em, but it was too late – they was outta sight. So I went back to the Just's place an saw Mr J cuttin firewood. He looked surprised when he saw I could hardly stand up. "What's the matter, Levi? Where's Ruth Ann?"

I was kinda dizzy so I sat on the ground fore I fell on it. "Kurt put me out, then grabbed Ruth Ann an took her away on his horse. We gotta go after em!"

Mr. J yelled, "He did what? You mean Kurt Johansson kidnapped Ruth Ann?"

"Yessir, that's exackly what I mean."

Mr. J ran into the cabin to tell Mrs. J what was goin on an where he was goin. When he came out his oldest son Josiah went to the barn an started saddlin two horses.

"Which way did they go, Levi.?"

"Toward town. The Johanssons live above their store, don't they?"

"Yep. You up to ridin?"

"I'll be ok. But first I'm gonna go by our camp an pick up Pa an Tom. It's on the way an Kurt seems like the type that won't give her up easy. The more folks we have the better chance we can get her outta there without a fight."

"All right, but I'll do whatever it takes to get my daughter back, even if it comes to that." He was lookin at the rifle I always carry on my saddle bag. Guess even peaceful has its limits.

Then Mr. J said "Josiah and I will wait for you and your folks out front of the store."

It didn't take long for Pa an Tom to mount up after I told em what had happened. We rode into town an found Mr J an Josiah where he said they'd be. The four of em walked up the steps an into the store. But I figgered there must be a back door, so I took the Kentucky an moseyed round that way. Tweren't long fore I heard a lotta yellin an scufflin inside the store. Soon, Kurt came backin out the door, draggin Ruth Ann with his arm round her neck. She was limp, like a rag doll, an her dress was half tore off.

Kurt was yellin, "Anyone comes near me I swear I'll choke her good. If I can't have her no one will!"

All of a sudden I membered that same kinda thing happenin on the Canal boat when that tattooed bum had his arm round her neck. I felt the same hard, cold anger as then, like I'd kill him if that's what it took to get her safe. I raised the Kentucky, but I knew I couldn't shoot fear I'd hit her steada him. So I turned it round, grabbed the barrel an swung it hard. The stock caught him square on the back a the head. He went down an stayed down.

Ruth Ann fell on toppa him so I picked her up an held her close til she came round, then set her down on the step. By then Kurt was tryin to sit up. I picked up the Kentucky, the right way this time, an aimed it straight at Kurt's face. I think, even now, I'da pulled the trigger if Ruth Ann hadn't stopped me.

"Levi! No! You'll ruin your whole life, and mine too!"

By now the others had come outta the back door an was yellin at me, but I kept the gun pointed at him. I weren't gonna shoot but I guess I kinda liked the look of fear an the way he had turned white as a sheet. After a while, I layed the rifle down, grabbed him by the hair and slammed my fist into his face. I ain't done many things that felt that good.

Mr. Just took Ruth Ann in his arms an held onto her like he'd never let go. But she finally got free an came over an kissed me. She said, "That's the second time you've saved me."

Mr J said "Levi, I don't know how to thank you. I was a fool about that boy. I should have listened to Ruth Ann when she told me what he was like. If it hadn't been for you and the butt end of that rifle, this could have had a real bad ending. I guess there are times when fighting back is the only answer."

"Well, sir, I'm just grateful it's over and she's ok. Like she told you fore, we really are in love an I will do anythin to keep her safe. Mebbe what you said to Ruth Ann is true -- violence is a built-in part a me, but I've only ever used it to help the people I love."

"That's good enough for me, Levi. I'm glad for you to see Ruth Ann anytime she wants you to."

Like I said at the start, I can't believe all that happened today.

The Bridesmaid

Tuesday, September 12

Pa said we'll be breakin camp an leavin here tomorrow, but he asked me to go an see if there was any mail fore we left. So I rode into the Lansing post office an there was a letter for him from Ma. He was groomin the horses when I got back so he asked me to read it to him. She wrote bout all the things been goin on in Groveland an wondered when we'd be gettin back there. But mostly it was to tell us that Sarah is gonna get married to William Russell in the spring. That weren't no surprise but it was good to see it's gonna happen. Them two seem like a great pair.

When I went to put the letter back in the envelope I saw there was another smaller one still inside. It said "To Ruth Ann from Sarah" an on the bottom was the word "Personal." That puzzled me. I knew them two had talked some but I didn't know they was close enough for "Personal." But it was fine by me – it gave me a reason to ride over to their place.

Mrs. Just was cleanin up after breakfast when I got there. She said "Well, hello Levi. Mr. Just told me what a brave thing you did yesterday saving Ruth Ann from that Johansson boy. I can't thank you enough."

"I'm glad we got there in time, Mrs. Just. That guy was mean clear through. Reason I came by is my Pa got a letter from Ma this mornin an inside was this personal note for Ruth Ann. Would you give it to her?"

"She's right out back, Levi, washing her hair. Why don't you give it to her? And before you leave, take some of these fried cakes. I just made a fresh batch and they should be cool in a while."

"Ruth Ann told me what a good baker you are, an I'd be mighty pleased to have some. Thanks!"

When I went out back she was bent over with her head under the well spout, tryin to pump with one hand an rub the soap outta her long hair with th'other. It was hangin down almost to the ground an water was runnin off it like a river. She looked so comical I almost laughed out loud, but then my brain kicked in. I decided to help instead, so I took the handle an started pumpin. She was so surprised she stood up sudden like an her hair fell in front of her face an water ran down all over her. She looked kinda mad til she saw it was me an started to laugh, not carin that she was getting soaked. I never saw such a beautiful sight, so I pulled her close an kissed her.

Lucky the note was in my back pocket so it didn't get wet. After I helped her dry her head I took it out an gave it to her. "This came in a letter from Ma to Pa. I figgered it might be important so I brought it right over."

She opened it an read it over a coupla times, then looked at me with her eyes real wide. "Levi, your sister Sarah's getting married and wants me to be a bridesmaid!"

I near fell over. Those two musta got a lot friendlier on the Canal boat than I spected. I said "That's a great idea Ruth Ann, but how you gonna get there? You ain't likely to travel that far on your own."

She said "Sarah says my folks are invited too, but I don't know if Papa will want to go away that long during planting season."

I thought that mebbe the only way it could happen is for me to come an get her. But I didn't say it out loud. If she goes an how she gets there is the Just's business, not mine, less I can help.

I waited in the yard while she went inside to finish dryin off an change her dress an whatever else women wear. She came back out lookin fresh an pretty as a daisy.

We went for a walk in the woods an sat on the same log as when Kurt Johansson jumped me, only this time he weren't out there.

We even did some talkin. She said she would work on her folks real hard to come to the weddin, even offer to double up on her chores if that would help. We was both excited bout the possibility that our families could get together.

Bout then Mrs. J stuck her head out the door an called "Ruth Ann, it's dinner time. You too, Levi, if you can stay."

"Thanks, Mrs Just -- I'd like to. Then I'll have to say goodbye to you all. We're leavin here early tomorrow mornin an we got lots to do this afternoon."

Ruth Ann's voice had kind of a hitch in it when she said "Oh, Levi, do you have to go so soon?"

"Fraid so. Pa wants to get back fore the early snowfall, an to help Matthew finish up the harvestin."

I reckon Mrs J is as good a cook as Ma, an that's sayin a lot. The dinner weren't fancy like that spread we had at the Bagley Inn – I knew the name of every dish. But it was just as good, an I guess I ate more'n my share.

An now came the hard part – sayin goodbye to Ruth Ann. We wandered off into the woods an sat on the same log again – it seemed to be our favorite talkin place. She promised to work on her folks to go to Sarah's weddin. Then I decided to jump in. "If your Pa says he can't come, I'd be glad to come an get you an your Ma."

"Oh, would you Levi? That would be wonderful!" Then she put her arms around my neck an kissed me. Well, that didn't help my leavin at all. Finally, tho, we went back to the cabin an I said goodbye to Mr an Mrs Just an Josiah an thanked em for the fine meal. She handed me a bag of her fried cakes too.

As I rode away, I looked back an saw all four of em wavin at me. I had the feelin that Mr J was finally gettin used to the idea that I might be round for a while

When I got back Pa asked me to answer Ma's letter an tell her all that's happened, since I ain't wrote in over a month. So I did that, tellin her bout findin nother cousin, Abraham, bout buildin our cabin, an bout seein the Justs again, specially Ruth Ann. But I didn't tell her bout our troubles with the Johansson family. That don't belong in a letter.

Then I said we's leavin tomorrow an should be home in bout a week.

The Indian Princess

Wednesday, September 13

This was nother one a them weird days.

On the way outta Lansing we dropped off the letter to Ma at the post office. Then we got on the Grand River Trail an headed east. This time it was just the three of us with Mike an Maggie pullin the wagon so we made pretty good time.

It was gettin on to supper time when we came on that same clearin where the Potawatamie attacked us. I wanted to keep on goin cause a what happened there. But Tom said "That tribe is always on the move – they probably aren't even around here now. And this time we'll post a guard and be on the lookout."

I weren't near so confident bout that, an Pa 'greed with me. He said "I'm not so sure they move round that much this time a year, Tom. Sides, I understand why Levi's not keen on stayin in a place where he darn near got killed." So we moved a few miles further up the trail an found a bigger clearin where we could see a long way off if anythin's comin. But I was still kinda skittish an told Pa an Tom I weren't gonna go wanderin into the woods to hunt somethin fresh. So we had last night's left over rabbit stew. After supper I was walkin over to a nearby stream to wash up when I heard a low growl off to my right. What I saw froze me in my tracks. There ain't s'posed to be many wolves left in Michigan, specially this far south, but this was sure nuff a livin, breathin wolf.

He weren't lookin at me, tho. He was lookin straight ahead an creepin toward a big sumac bush on the edge a the clearin. An crouchin behind it was a young girl with a buncha colored feathers in her hair. She was whimperin an shakin like she knew the wolf was gonna jump her. When he was bout ten feet away from the girl he stopped and crouched real low to the ground, like a cat does just afore it leaps.

Right bout then I was real glad I never go anywhere without the Kentucky. The wolf was bout fifty yards away, an just as he jumped I swung the gun up to my left shoulder an fired. He was in midair when that .50 caliber ball hit him in the neck an spun him clear round. He dropped to the ground a few feet from her an lay real still. The girl sat watchin the wolf for several minutes, then jumped up, raced across the field an threw herself onto me, sobbin real hard.

When Pa an Tom heard the rifle shot, they came runnin over from camp to see what happened. First they looked at the dead wolf, then at the girl clingin to me like a vine. Tom said, "Looks like you saved that girl from a bad mauling, Levi. You know, I think that's an Ottawa head dress, an those aren't ordinary feathers. This girl may be royalty in her tribe."

Then he spoke to her in the same language he used when he got the potion for Abraham. But she surprised us by answering in English, saying "My father is chief of our tribe. He will be angry with me for coming out here alone, but he will want to thank you for saving me from wolf."

Just then, three Indian men came out of the woods, notched arrows in their bows and pointed them at us. The biggest one shouted somethin at us. Tom said it was Algonquin an meant "Let her go or we shoot!" The girl jumped up an started yellin back. Tom said she was tellin him how I saved her from the wolf. The braves lowered their bows an the girl ran into the arms of the big Indian. She talked for several minutes, wavin her arms an pointin at me, I guess tellin him all bout it.

The big man musta been her father. He walked over to us an said somethin that Tom repeated in English. "The chief wants to apologize for threatening to shoot at us, and to thank you, Levi, for saving his daughter. He's inviting us to come to their village so they can show their gratitude.

Tom said "We'd better go because refusing could be insulting. After all, we're in their territory and should respect their customs."

So that's what we did. We went with the chief an his daughter an the two braves through the woods for a coupla miles to a big clearin near a lake. There was huts an wigwams an at least thirty people – men an women, all ages from babies to gray haired.
When we entered the village they all stopped what they were doin an looked at the chief, waitin for him to tell em bout us.

The chief called a young brave bout my age over to his side an said somethin to him, then he spoke to the entire tribe. The young man said to us "My father want me to tell you what he says to his people. He tells them of your brave act in killing wolf and saving Ayiana from his terrible teeth. He said you must have been visited by spirit of great marksman to shoot like that. He asks wife to prepare feast for our families to thank you."

After the chief had finished talkin, Tom asked the boy his name. "I am called Chogan -- it is Algonquin for Blackbird. My sister's name, Ayiana, means Eternal Blossom. Ottawa, Potawatomie and Algonquin are bonded together as Council of Three Fires. We have mostly same language and customs."

Course, the chief's wigwam was the biggest one in the village an he called us over to sit round the fire in front of it with him, his son Chogan an the elders of the tribe. The meal was good tho I didn't know what I was eatin. I hoped it would stay where I put it. After, I was fraid they'd pass round that pipe they was smoking -- an they sure nuff did. It was bout the worse thing I ever smelled. I managed to puff it without inhalin much but it still made me gag an cough. They tried to hide their smiles so's not to embarrass the hero of the day.

It was startin to get dark an we figgered to say goodbye an get back to our camp, but the chief had other plans. Seems like this was dancin time.

Bout six of the women was dressed real fancy from head to foot, an while some of the braves beat on their tom-toms the women danced in a big circle round the council fire. Then Ayiana, the princess, grabbed me by the hand, pulled me up an started to dance round me. I didn't know what to do so I just stood there like a dummy while the whole tribe started chantin an clappin their hands with the drum beat.

Finally, the dancin an the chantin an the clappin stopped an we all sat back down. Tom leaned over to me an said "There's an old Indian custom that when you save someone's life they belong to you. I think you just got yourself engaged."

Well, let me tell you, if I ever felt like runnin, now was the time. I reached for the Kentucky an started to get up. But Tom put a hand on my arm an said "Wait, Levi, let me see what I can do."

He went over to the chief an his family an all of em jawed back an forth for quite a while. I could see it was gettin kinda intense now an then but finally Tom came back an said "I told them that you were already engaged to a white girl in Lansing and were going to get married next spring in Oakland County. They asked me lots of questions about you and her, and finally agreed that the first promise should stand. But Ayiana would like to speak to you before you leave."

She walked away from her family over toward the woods an I followed her. She stopped an turned to me an took my hand. "Levi, I am most grateful for what you did. I know it is our custom that I should become your bride, but I think that is not fair to you or to me. I am glad my father released us from it and that you are engaged to another woman. I hope you will be very happy."

"Ayiana, I'm sure you'll find someone among your own people who's better for you than me. An I hope you'll be happy too."

Fore we left the chief gathered his people round him an told Tom he wanted to give me a gift. What he handed me was bout a foot long an wrapped in a leather skin. As I opened it, they was all kinda smilin an when I saw it I knew why. It was the peace pipe we had all been smokin.

When me, Pa an Tom walked out of the village I looked back. The chief an his family was wavin to us.

Groveland

Thursday, September 14

It's good to be back. I'm writin this in the kitchen at Rachel an Matthew's place. We made right good time on the trail after we left the Indian camp. The ground was pretty dry an Mike an Maggie pulled hard all the way. They seemed to know they was headed home.

This was the first time Ma an Pa been apart for so long, an I could see they was both mighty glad to see each other again. I 'magain Sarah's glad too, but she was so busy gettin ready for her weddin she didn't spend a lotta time on us.

But the biggest news is that Rachel's gonna have nother baby! She's guessin it'll be coupla months fore Sarah's weddin but who knows? Mebbe the baby has other plans. Course Matthew hopes it's a boy so's he can teach him huntin an fishin an, later on, farmin. An little Sarah Jane says she wants a brother.

Tonight after supper the whole passel of us sat round the fireplace while me an Pa told bout all we did out west. Ma specially wanted to hear bout me gettin shot by the Indians an how the vet saved my life. Then Pa told bout buyin the land an findin a new cousin, Abraham squattin on it. Then he said me an Tom saved him from dyin a that ague fever an now he's gonna finish up the inside of the cabin this winter.

Sarah wanted to know all bout Ruth Ann an if she would be comin for the weddin to be a bridesmaid. I said I didn't know -- she wants to come but it's up to her folks. Then I told em bout Kurt Johansson an what he tried to do to Ruth Ann an how her Pa helped us get her back.

That's when Sarah asked "Levi, are you planning to marry that girl? Cause if you aren't, you're crazy!"

I said "I'd sure like to someday if she'll have me."

"Oh, she'll have you. She's made that pretty clear to me."

"You mean you an her been talkin bout us gettin married?"

"Course we have, silly. Women always talk about things like that. She was even trying on your last name – Ruth Ann Broas. Women always do that too!"

Well, that got me to thinkin in a whole new way. Sure, after that stuff with the Ottawa princess I'd joked in a letter to Ruth Ann that we oughtta think bout gettin engaged or I'd be in trouble with the Indians. But 'cordin to Sarah, here we was practickly hitched! Guess I still got a lot to learn bout women.

Sunday, November 7

Today we met up with the Russells after church services an Ma said Rachel was plannin a big family Thanksgivin dinner. She asked Betsey if they'd like to come an that Amos an Esther was invited too. Groveland is bout halfway tween Flint an Pontiac an would be a good place to get both sides a the family together. Course Mrs. R was real pleased an said she'd write a letter to Amos an Esther right away so they could plan on it.

While that was goin on Pa, Mr Russell an Matthew was talkin bout what to plant next spring an where to plant it. Matthew's farm is a couple years old so he's already into rotatin crops. But Mr R's is brand new an the ground here in Michigan is different from what he had in New York so he was askin Matthew for advice.

Sarah an William seemed to disappear for a while. When they came back her face was kinda flushed.

Monday, November 13

This mornin Ma an Rachel said they needed to go into Pontiac to shop for some extra dishes an flatware for Thanksgivin dinner.

An Matthew said he needs a new ox yoke cause one broke durin the harvest. Chores are light round the farm now so Pa an Matthew said we could all go in the wagon. I wanted some powder an shot for the Kentucky an to mail a letter to Ruth Ann.

We was almost to the Pontiac General Store when we saw a man that looked familiar on a big black stallion. I was tryin to think of his name when Pa called out.

"Judge Bagley, member us? My family 'n me stopped at your Inn last spring."

Then it came back to me – that dinner I can't never forget. The Judge looked at us kinda confused but suddenly his face lit up an he rode over to our wagon. "Mr. and Mrs. Broas! Is that really you?"

"Yessir, it sure is. You member Levi? An this is my daughter Rachel an my son-in-law Matthew Coons. They're the ones I was after when you told me how to get to Groveland."

Matthew spoke up an said, "Pleased to meet you, your honor. I used to train horses in New York, an I think I've seen some of the best, but that stallion is a real stand-out. Have you had him long?"

"This is Justice, my pride and joy. I raised him from a colt and he seems to understand almost everything I say. Well, isn't this a coincidence that we should meet again! What brings you all to Pontiac?"

Pa said, "The ladies are shoppin for some things for Thanksgivin. They're puttin on dinner for the whole family. I s'pose your Inn will be real busy that day?"

"No, actually we're closed both Thursday and Friday. I gave my staff those days off so they could celebrate with their own families."

"Well, that's mighty nice of you, Judge. But at least it will give you a chance to be with your family."

"I don't have any family around here, Charles. I lost my wife two years ago and our kids are still back east. So I'm planning to try out some special recipies on myself. I like to cook and the Inn kitchen is usually too busy for me to do much of that."

At this point Ma looked at Rachel an she nodded her head. Then Ma said, "Judge Bagley, we'd be mighty pleased if you'd join our family for Thanksgivin. It won't be near as fancy as the meals you serve at your Inn but we'd love to have you."

"You know, Mrs. Broas, that's an offer I can't refuse. The chance to sit down to dinner with a real family is something I haven't had in quite a while. Thank you so much for inviting me."

Then Pa said, "An bring your overnight stuff Judge, it's a four or five hour ride an you don't wanna try goin back in the dark, specially if the weather's bad."

"You know, I guess I'd forgotten what real country hospitality is. This sounds like it would be a lot better than spending the holiday alone in a deserted Inn. I'll be happy to come, and thank you again."

Matthew told him their farm is on Old Mill road, east of Sagainaw Trail. Then he said, "I fixed the sign at the entrance. Come anytime on Thursday mornin. We'll have dinner bout two o'clock."

"I'll be there. Let's go, Justice." He turned his horse an rode off. Then Pa an Matthew went to Michaelmann's Farm Supply an I walked over to the Post Office. The postman took my letter, then he said, "I see you are a Broas. Do you know somebody named Charles Broas?'

"Sure, that's my Pa. If there's a letter for him I can take it."

Turns out it was from Erastus Higbee in Orleans. When I gave it to Pa an he started to read it he got a real worried look on his face. He said, "Abraham had trouble with the chimney. Looks like some animals built a nest in it while the weather was warm an the first time he lit a fire everythin backed up an filled the cabin with smoke. Erastus says that was a month ago an the place still smells. But other'n that he done a good job on the inside."

Thanksgiving

Thursday, November 23

This was nother one a them special days. It got goin real early when the women got up to start the cookin. Course a lot a the bakin, like bread an rolls, had been done yesterday. But a turkey that big had to be in the oven for a long time, so the smell a that roastin bird is what got me up. Then they started in on the pies – pumpkin -- four of em. I kept walkin back an forth through the kitchen, dippin in the fillin with my finger til Ma whacked it with a spatula.

But the weather almost ruined the whole day. A storm had been buildin since early mornin. Tweren't a tornado, I'da known that for sure. But the winds comin straight across the fields from the west was the strongest I ever seen. There was trees an hay bundles an pieces of outbuildins flyin through the air like we was at war. Pa an Matthew thought they had got all the livestock into the barn, but I swear I saw a chicken go by at round fifty miles an hour.

The women had got dinner ready by two clock, but it was pushin three an Judge Bagley still weren't here. Pa said we better go look for him, so we got Mike an Maggie outta the barn an headed down Sagainaw Trail, tryin to stay in the saddle gainst that awful wind. We'd almost got to Clarkston when we saw a man afoot, strugglin up the trail, holdin onto his hat an a cloth sack. It were him alright, but he didn't look very judge-like.

Pa got him up behind him on Mike an we rode back to the farm without even tryin to talk. When we got in the house he told us what had happened. He said he saw a tree startin to fall toward em so he pulled hard on the reins but it was too late. It missed him but came down on Justice's neck an broke it. He couldn't do nothin for him in the storm, but figgered he was probly dead anyway. He said he'd bury Justice on the way home tomorrow. The Judge was really sad cause that big stallion had been with him since it was born.

Then he said to me an Pa, "I'm really grateful that you came for me in this awful weather. Just before you got there I was about to give up walking. I planned to sit on the lee side of a big tree and wait for either the storm to let up or the Lord to come and get me."

Dinner was late but that didn't spoil it none, least not so's you could tell. Everyone ate like it was the first time in a week. Even in that storm the Judge had hung on to the sack he was carryin, an after dinner he opened it. There was sachet for the ladies an Irish whiskey for the men. The sachet was kinda damp from the storm but the whiskey made it through just fine.

After everythin was cleaned up people gathered round the fireplace in the sittin room an just talked. Sarah told me later that the Judge got her an William aside an asked bout their weddin plans. She told him they had most everythin set cept for one a the bridesmaids -- Levi's Lansing friend Ruth Ann Just. She didn't know if her family could make it. He 'lowed as how if they was really in love she'd find a way. I sure hope he's right.

The Invitation

Friday, November 24

The wind finally died down bout midnight an everyone got to sleep after that. This mornin at breakfast Matthew said he had a horse that he could spare an that Judge Bagley should keep him as long as he wants. Pa said, "Levi, let's me an you ride as far as Clarkston an help the Judge bury his horse."

So that's what we did. That stallion sure was a heavy beast. It was all the three of us could do to drag him a few feet off the trail to the pit we had dug. The Judge got kinda choked up when we buried the horse, but then he straightened up an said, "I can't thank you enough for all you've done for me. These two days have made me feel like I've been part of a family again, and I'd like to do something for you. Christmas is a pretty special time at the Bagley Inn. We have a church service on Christmas Eve and the next day sleigh rides and caroling and Santa has gifts for all the kids. I'd really like it if you would all bring your children down on Friday and stay the weekend as my guests."

Pa was caught with his tongue kinda tied up. Finally he said, "Well, gee, thanks Judge, that sounds really nice. I'll talk it over with Catherine an the rest a the family. I don't know if they had other plans for the holidays but I'll bet they'd rather do this."

"Well, I hope you all can come. And Levi, after dinner yesterday your sister Sarah was telling me that she will be married in the spring. And she said that you are practically engaged to one of her bridesmaids, a young lady from Lansing."

"I'd sure like to be, Judge, but I ain't really asked her yet."

"Oh? And when do you plan to do that?"

"I don't rightly know. It ain't like she lives next door, an it don't seem proper to do somethin like that in a letter."

"Well, I have a suggestion. I have to be in Lansing during Christmas week for a meeting with the Supreme Court justice who oversees the Detroit district. If your lady friend and her family would like to join us for that weekend I'd be happy to bring them back to the Inn with me. We could all enjoy Christmas together, and then you could propose in proper fashion."

"You'd really do that? Wow! That'd be the best possible thing I could imagaine!"

"Why don't I prepare an invitation asking them to be my guests for the weekend and then you could enclose it in your own letter to the young lady. And tell them that I'll arrange transportation back home for them. I'm also planning to invite the Russell family to come down so Sarah and William can be together."

"I don't know what to say, Judge Bagley, cept thank you!"

The Ring

Saturday, November 25

When we got home last night I was too het up to write in the journal, but I gotta get this down.

Soons we walked through the door Pa started tellin Ma an Rachel bout the Judge's invitation for us to spend Christmas weekend at the Bagley Inn. Just then Sarah an Matthew came in the room so Pa told the whole thing again an everybody got real excited. Rachel was a little worried bout travelin in her condition but Ma thought she wouldn't be too far along for that.

Then I said, "An there's more, lots more. The Judge said he's goin to Lansing that week an would bring the Justs back with him if they wanna come for Christmas!" Everyone, but specially Sarah, looked at me an she asked, "Whose idea was that, Levi?" I said it were the Judge's but I was all for it.

Later on I got Ma an Pa alone an told them that if the Justs come I was plannin to ask Ruth Ann to marry me. I don't think they was really surprised, but they acted like it. Then Ma said "Levi, I want you to have my engagement ring. It's been in the Broas family for a long time an now it's your turn."

I said, "Oh, Ma I can't take that."

"Yes, you can. The stone in this ring is a perfect blue-white diamond. It was bought by your great-grandpa Pieter for great-grandma Elizabeth. He asked her to make sure it would stay in the Broas family, so it came down to me from your grandma Phebe. Now I'm gonna go get the box it came in when Pieter bought it. That's been handed down too."

When she came back she kept the ring on but handed me a little ole red velvet box with the name "Tiffany, London." She said, "Keep this in your pocket when you ask Ruth Ann to marry you. If she says 'yes' give her the ring in the box an tell her what I've told you bout it. If she says 'no' leave it in your pocket and give it back to me until you find someone else."

The Gifts

Friday, December 22

This was a time of gettin ready for Christmas at Judge Bagley's Inn. Everybody wanted to give him somethin an Pa started right after Thanksgivin by decidin to make him a gavel. When Matthew bought his farm there was a rusted old foot-pedal lathe in the barn. Me an Pa cleaned an oiled it so it worked almost like new. We couldn't find no shapin tools but back home Pa was a real good blacksmith so he made some from a broken pitchfork.

We cut a middlin-size branch from one a the walnut trees that grow near the creek an then set to work. With me pumpin the foot-pedal Pa was able to concentrate on the shapers an fore long he had roughed out both the head an the handle. Then we switched jobs an I sanded em down til they was silky smooth.

After joinin the two pieces we shellacked it so it had a nice dark shine. Then Pa hammered a small piece a tin good an flat an scratched the Judge's name an date on it,

Judge Amasa Bagley
from the Broas Family
Christmas 1837

Then he fastened it to the head a the gavel with four nails so small you could hardly see em. Ma took a old shoe box an lined it with some cotton an satin cloth shaped so the gavel fit in just right. Then she decorated the box with paper an trimmins.

Rachel had noticed when the Judge came up to the house for Thanksgivin dinner he was tryin to hold onto his hat in the wind. It gave her the idea that he could use a wool cap an mebbe a scarf too.

Now Matthew has eight white sheep an two black ones. They was sheared in April an the fleece was washed an combed but not spun into yarn yet. So Rachel got the spinnin wheel outta the storage room an taught Sarah how to make yarn. When they had got a few yards of black yarn they each took a roll of it an started in to knit. The cap was harder so Rachel took that an she got Sarah started on the scarf.

When Ma saw what they were doin she said, "That's real nice, girls, but I think he needs gloves too." Rachel said, "Sure he does Ma, but I don't know how to knit gloves."

"Why don't I make him a pair of mittens. They're warmer than gloves an easier to knit. I made lots of em for you kids cause you kept losin em." So she took some yarn an set in to make mittens for the Judge.

Then little Sarah Jane went up to Rachel an asked, "Momma, what are you doin with them sticks an that fuzzy string?" "We're knittin Christmas presents for Judge Bagley, honey. You member him don't you? The big man that was here for Thanksgivin dinner?"

"He was nice. I wanna make him somethin too."

"Well, you're not old enuff to knit. Why don't you draw him a picture with the charcoal sticks Daddy got you for your birthday?"

"Okay. What should I draw?"

"Well, the Judge's horse was hurt on his way to our house. Why don't you draw a picture of a horse?"

So Sarah Jane sat on the floor with paper an her charcoal sticks an drew what to her was a picture of a big black horse. Then she asked me, "Uncle Levi will you write 'Justice' on the bottom?" She musta membered when the Judge was tellin us bout his stallion an how bad he felt for losin him.

Our Christmas gifts to the Judge weren't worth much money but they had a lotta heart in em.

Christmas Eve

Sunday, December 24

Pa's blacksmithin came in handy again. Last week him an Matthew took the wheels off the wagon an made sleigh runners to fit on the underside. That was good timin cause it's been snowin all week an by now there's bout a foot a the stuff. Ma an Rachel made strings of bells and strung em on Mike an Maggie with some bows an ribbons. When Pa saw that he said, "If they had horns they could pass for Santa's reindeer."

Today started real early cause it's bout a five hour trip to the Inn. With seven people an some dress-up clothes an all the presents the wagon was pretty full. But it didn't seem to bother Mike an Maggie, cause it's probly easier pullin a sleigh on snow than a wagon on wheels that keep diggin in the dirt.

Time we got goin the sun was up an the air was gettin warmer. The Judge had written the Russells invitin them for the weekend too but Mrs. R wrote back sayin they were goin to Flint to be with Amos an his family. But she said that William would be glad to join em, so on the way down we stopped at their place to pick him up. He sat next to Sarah an they looked at each other like there weren't no one else around.

We made good time down to Pontiac but then with all the horse an buggy traffic in town the road got real mushy an one a the runners got stuck in a big rut. Mike an Maggie pulled an pulled but it wouldn't come out. So Pa said "We gotta get some a the weight outta this wagon an give it a good shove." Ma took the reins an all the men got out an pushed an sloshed through the mud an wet snow. With Mike an Maggie strainin hard as they could we got it unstuck, but our clothes was a awful mess.

We was back on the trail an movin ok when Ma yelled what for her was a string a cuss words. "Darn it all to heck! We was all nice an clean, but now we're gonna get to the Bagley Inn lookin even messier'n we did the first time we was here. An them high falutin women is gonna push up their noses at us again."

But Pa said, "This time we'll go in the back way an mebbe the Judge'll find us a place to clean up fore we go out front."

We didn't get to the Inn til after noon. Course the place looked real different from when we was here in May, all decorated up for Christmas, an there was lotsa wagons an buggies in the parkin space. Pa drove the wagon round to the back near the kitchen entrance an went in an asked if he could talk to Judge Bagley. The fancy-pants who served our dinner last spring recognized him.

He said, "Welcome to Bagley Inn, Mr. Broas. My name is Jefferson Brogan. The Judge told us to expect your family. As you may know, he had a meeting with a Supreme Court Justice on Friday. It's almost a two-day trip to Lansing, so he left here on Wednesday, and expected to be back at the Inn by this afternoon." Then Pa told him what we was after an why some of us was so dirty. "I'm sure we can get you a place to refresh and clean up. Please come with me to the staff quarters."

So he took us to a big house across the lane. He said, "This is home to about seventy people. We handle all the business of running Bagley Inn -- cooks, housekeepers, waiters, maintenance, and even some of their families. The Inn is very busy right now so the house is quite empty. Help yourselves to the facilities, and just leave your soiled clothes in this hamper. We'll have them laundered by tomorrow morning."

Well, that was quite an offer cause he seen us an knew what was gonna go into that hamper. Lucky Ma insisted we all take a extra set of clean clothes. So after we was all slicked up again Pa went back to the kitchen an found Mr Brogan. (I can't call him fancy-pants no more cause he's been pretty nice to us.) He said, "Now I'll take you to your rooms. The Judge has reserved one of the guest suites on the top floor for your family. It has a nice view of the Rouge River and in clear weather you can even see the lake district to the west."

The climb up all them stairs to the third floor was kinda hard for Ma but when we got to the rooms she said it sure was worth it. There was two bedrooms an a sittin parlor an a small room with. a water closet, just like the one we had last spring.

While all this was goin on I could hardly stand still. Ruth Ann had written me to say that her folks had agreed to the Judge's offer to bring em to the Inn. So I couldn't hardly wait to see her. An that little red box was burnin a hole in my pocket.

It was bout then that I was lookin out the window an saw a fancy carriage pulled by two big horses come into the lot an five people got out. I don't member when I started breathin again cause the first an only one I saw was Ruth Ann. Good thing there weren't nobody tween me an the door cause I'da knocked em down.

Course by the time I got to the lobby I had slowed down considable cause I didn't want nobody to think I was anxious or anythin. Then I picked her outta the crowd. She was standin by the entrance with her folks, lookin round at all the people. Her coat was long an had a furry hood that surrounded her face like a halo. When she spotted me she smiled an we started movin toward each other. I wondered if she wanted to kiss me as much as I wanted to kiss her, but instead I squeezed her hand an said, "Hi Ruth Ann, it's sure good to see you." Nother one a them romantic speeches I'm famous for.

She squeezed back an said, "I've missed you so much, Levi. I can't believe Judge Bagley brought us all the way here to spend Christmas weekend. What a special friend your family has made!"

"He sure is that. At Thanksgivin when Sarah told him bout us it seemed like he was jumpin at the chance to get our families together."

Just then Ma an Pa came down the stairs an both families started talkin in the middle of that crowded lobby like there weren't nobody else around. Then the Judge came in an walked over to us. He said, "Well, hello there, folks. I'm so glad you could all come to celebrate Christmas at the Inn. I think this can be a memorable weekend for us all." As he said that he turned his head so no one else could see him wink at me.

Then he waved at Mr.Brogan who was standin to one side. He turned to the Justs an said, "Jefferson will take you folks to your rooms in the suite next to the Broas's. I'm sure you'll enjoy the view from up there. The Christmas Eve service starts at eight o'clock, so why don't we meet for dinner about six. That should give everyone time to rest and refresh after this long day of travel."

Ma an Pa stayed downstairs an just moseyed around but me an Sarah an William went up with the Justs to help em get settled in their rooms. I was able to get Mr J aside in one a the bedrooms an I said, "Mr Just, I'm sure you know I'm deep in love with your daughter an I wanna marry her. I ain't rich or handsome an I don't talk as good as I should, but I'll spend my life tryin to make her happy. I'd sure like it if you said it was ok with you an Mrs J."

He didn't answer right away but stood there lookin at me like he was decidin what to do. Then he smiled an said, "Levi, I had serious misgivings about you for a while but that's all in the past. And Mrs Just has been arguing your case for months. We both would be honored to have you as part of our family." He shook my hand an I said, "Thanks, Mr Just, you won't regret this, I promise."

When they was finished puttin stuff away they all started to go downstairs, but Sarah pulled me over to our room an said, "Did you bring the ring? When are you gonna ask her? Are you gonna give her the box too? Do you want me to be there?"

I said, "Hold on, Sarah. I'm just as excited as you, but don't rush me. I wanna do this right an I'm tryin to stay calm so's I don't say somethin stupid. An no, I don't need you to be there!"

William an the Justs was goin toward the stairway when Ruth Ann saw us. She came into the room an said with a smile on her face, "What are you two up to? You look like you're plotting some big scheme."

That's when Sarah said, "Wait for me folks, I'm going down too." Mrs Just smiled at her an said, "Come along, Sarah, I expect those two would like some time alone."

When it was just the two of us I took Ruth Ann in my arms an for a few minutes we tried to make up for a lotta lost time. Then I put my hands on her shoulders an moved her away a bit. I took the little red box outta my pocket an got down on one knee. Suddenly she got all red an teary. I'm sure she knew what was comin.

"Ruth Ann, I fell in love with you when I first saw you on the Canal boat at Rochester. I stepped back to let your family come up the gangplank an you said 'Thank you'. That did it. I knew right then that I wanted to marry you someday. Well, now I want you to know it too."

I opened the box an said, "This ring was bought by my great-grandpa Pieter for great-grandma Elizabeth, an it's been handed down to the first son in each family ever since.

"Ruth Ann, will you wear it, an will you marry me?"

She dropped to her knees an said, "Oh yes, Levi. Yes, yes, yes, I'll marry you!"

I slipped the ring on her finger an it fit just fine – like it was made for her. We stayed there kissin til our knees got sore. Then we went downstairs to tell everybody what we done.

Can't write no more -- gotta finish this tomorrow

Christmas Day

Monday, December 25

I guess the dinner last night was great but I don't member much bout the food cause it was mostly a celebration for Ruth Ann an me. She held her left hand out to her Ma first, then so everyone else could see the ring. Then I passed the box round the table. Ma told Mrs J bout how the ring was a old family heirloom that had come down from my great grand folks. The Judge winked at me again an said how glad he was that we could get together at his Inn for the holiday.

Sarah asked Ruth Ann when the weddin would be, but she said we hadn't even talked about that yet. Then Sarah took William's hand an said, "Why don't you make it a double wedding with William and me?" Everybody stopped talkin an looked at us. Ruth Ann was kinda flustered an muttered somethin like, "We'll have to think about that."

If I'da been next to Sarah I'da kicked her. Puttin Ruth Ann on the spot like that fronta everybody weren't very nice. But Sarah's always been kinda pushy bout tellin other people what to do. After dinner I got Ruth Ann aside an said, "Don't let Sarah push you into anythin. If you want a double weddin that's ok with me, but it's gonna be our day an it's gonna be the way we want it, not nobody else," Seems like she relaxed then an said, "Things are happening so fast Levi. I love your sister an maybe it's a good idea, but we need time to think and make our own plans."

The Christmas Eve service was real nice. The boy's choir from one a the churches in Pontiac sang carols an Reverend Gordon read from the Good Book bout Christ's birth. At the end he told everybody in the place bout our engagement an they all turned round an clapped their hands. It was real embarrasin.

But the rest a the evenin was for the kids an Ruth Ann was glad to have the attention offa her. There was bout twenty young ones at the Inn an Jefferson had em all gather round the fireplace. He started tellin stories bout Christmas when he was a kid. He was in the middle a one bout puttin horns on his Pa's horse when we heard a loud "Ho, Ho, Ho" from the next room. Everybody turned round an there was Santa comin in with a big sack over his shoulder. That kinda ended the story-tellin.

Santa took a chair by the fireplace an put his sack on the floor. Then one at a time he had each kid sit on his lap an tell who they was an what was the one thing they wanted most for Christmas. He made a big show of thinkin hard and then lookin through his sack til he came up with a package that had the kid's name on it. An like magic, it was just what they had asked for!

Well, for mosta those kids that put Santa just bout one step below God. After Santa left they started askin lotsa questions like, "How did he do that so quick?" an, "How did he get the toys without leavin here?"

Later, when the Judge came back in the room, he said, "What did I miss? Where did you get all these presents?" The little ones started yellin all at once bout Santa an his magic sack. Then he said, "Gee, I sure picked the wrong time to leave the room! Maybe he would have had a present for me too!" At that everybody laughed.

It was the kid's bedtime, but Rachel let Sarah Jane stay up a little longer.

Then Ma said, "Judge Bagley, I think now's a good time to give you the presents we have for you. They ain't fancy but we made em ourselves." She gave him the package that had the cap, scarf an mittens an when he opened it she said, "These is from the Coons sheep an the Broas women. Wish you'da had em when you came up through that awful storm on Thanksgivin."

"Oh my, thank you so much, ladies! I've never had anything like this. I'm sure they'll get a lot of use in our Michigan winters."

Then Pa gave him the box with the gavel. Fore he opened it Pa said, "This is from Levi, Matthew an me, Judge. I'm sure you've got a better one but this can be kind of a backup case your's gets lost or busted."

The Judge opened the box, picked up the gavel an just sat there feelin it an lookin at it. Finally he said "Charles, this is the finest gavel I've ever seen. My other one just got lost! Thank you all"

Then Sarah Jane said, "Is it my turn now, mommy?"

"Yes, honey, it's your turn now."

She handed him her picture an said, "I drawed this for you cause your horse got dead. I hope you like it Mr. Judge."

He tried to talk a few times but then he stopped tryin. He weren't the Judge no more. He reached for Sarah Jane and hugged her close. Finally he said, "I'll put this on the wall in my bedroom so it's the first thing I see every morning and the last thing I see at night. Thank you dear Sarah Jane, for helping me remember what a fine horse Justice was."

*　　*　　*

This mornin most a the families with kids was sleepin late, so the Inn was kinda quiet when I went down to breakfast. But Ruth Ann had beaten me there, an it looked like we had a chance to talk, just the two of us. After I got my eggs from the buffet she took me over to a table by the window.

"Levi, this ring is so beautiful. I just love it, and you for giving it to me." Then she said, "Now that we're alone, let's talk about wedding plans. With everything that happened yesterday, I had trouble sleeping last night. So I got to thinking about Sarah's suggestion of a double wedding. Yesterday you said it was ok with you if I wanted to. Do you really feel that way or were you just trying to calm me down?

"I guess it was a little a both, Ruth Ann. I could see that you was feelin like you might be gettin pushed into somethin fore you'd had a chance to think bout it. Far as I'm concerned we could take our vows front of a country preacher. But I know women like to look back on their weddin as a lot more'n that, with all their family an friends there. An a double ceremony would sure be somethin to look back on! It's ok with me if you really want it. "

"Then lets talk about that with our folks. After all, they should be part of this decision if it's going to be such a big affair." So we left it there for now.

The Judge weren't kiddin when he said they do sleigh rides round here. There's all kinds a trails in the fields and woods behind the Inn. Soon everybody was up an fed he told the kids to get bundled up cause it gets mighty cold ridin over them hills in the snow.

When Mike an Maggie saw the Judge's horses bein hitched up to a big hay-ride wagon they started fidgetin an pawin the ground. Guess they knew somethin was up an couldn't wait for the grooms to get our wagon out an hook them up too. Ruth Ann an me watched the kids an some a the parents pile into both wagons an off they went.

When we went back inside Ma an Pa an the Justs was sittin round the fire. I guess they was chattin bout me an Ruth Ann cause they stopped talkin soons they saw us. After we sat down Ruth Ann said, "We're glad you're all here because we want to talk to you about our wedding, and we are really confused. We have to decide what kind of ceremony, who to invite, where to have it and who to ask officiate with the vows and a lot of other things. Honestly, we don't know what to do."

I said, "We could save everyone a lotta trouble by just runnin off to a Justice a the Peace in Pontiac or Detroit. But I don't spec you'd be real happy bout that, an its probly not the kinda weddin we'd wanna look back on. So instead, we could have a small weddin in a church with just our families."

Then Ruth Ann jumped in, "Or we could do what Sarah said and make it a double wedding with her and William. But that's a really big affair and probably very expensive. So we need to know how you folks feel because you're a big part of this and we want you to be happy about it too."

Mrs Just said, "That's what we were discussing before you came in. We sure don't want you running off to a Justice of the Peace. Mr Just and I agreed that if you two and Sarah and William would like a double wedding we'll go along with it. But it's really a decision for your family Levi, because with both you and Sarah involved it's more of a burden on them than it is on us."

Then Ma spoke up. "Ya know, it's probably no more work or cost than two separate weddins, mebbe even less. 'Sides, the chance to see two of our kids married at the same time don't come along more'n once in a lifetime. Pa an me are agreed if it's what you four want."

Bout now Ruth Ann was startin to tear up. She went over to Ma an Mrs J an hugged em both. Then she said, "Oh, thank you! I guess this is what I've wanted all along but was afraid to admit it even to myself. I haven't known Sarah very long but I think we've gotten really close, and being married together would kind of seal our friendship."

Pa's always been the practical one. He said, "First, fore we go any further, mebbe you two should check with Sarah an William to be sure they *both* want to do it this way. Then if they do, you four got a lotta other things to decide, like, who, where an when. But mebbe we should let all that wait til after dinner." I kinda chuckled to myself, cause I knew there ain't many things more important to Pa than mealtime.

Sarah an William had gone with the kids on the sleigh ride, so when they came back the first thing Ruth Ann did was run up to her an give her a big hug. I guess Sarah knew right away what it was about an she said, "We're getting married together!"

Just then Judge Bagley came in an heard what Sarah said. He went over to the two girls an congratulated them an said, "I had a hunch this might happen. It's one of the reasons I wanted to get your families together. And if you decide you want the weddings here in our chapel you'll all be my guests. Just let me know when you plan to have it and we'll reserve the date."

The Dance

After supper that evening, but fore anyone left the dinin room, Mr. Brogan said, "One of our customs at the Inn is the Christmas Day dance. Every year we choose a traditional dance from a different country and our very talented musicians learn the music. For this year we picked the good old U S A, mostly because Mr Wes Cody is one of our guests. He is one of the best square dance callers east of the Mississippi.

"So tonight at seven o'clock you're all invited to the reception hall for a good old-fashioned hoe-down. Dress is casual, in fact gingham and jeans are recommended. Just be sure to wear comfortable shoes!"

Well, I never seen such change in a place. All them stuffed shirts an high-falutin ladies was gone an in their place was real, down to earth folks. The callin an dancin went on til almost midnight, with everybody swingin partners an dosado-in. Even some a the older kids got in on it.

When we started out the couples in our square was Ma with Mr J, Pa with Mrs J, William an Ruth Ann, Sarah an me. But after a while the caller had us mixin it up with other squares. Ma an me got put in a bunch with Mrs Ann Walton, the lady that snubbed us last spring when we first stopped at the Inn. Turned out she was a real pro at square dancin an was downright pleasant to us this time. Guess that's what dancin can do to people.

It was after eleven o'clock when Mr. Brogan took the stage an thanked everybody for comin. Then he said there'd be one last dance, a slow one for couples only. So we all paired up an I got a chance to dance with Ruth Ann alone stead a givin her away to some other guy. I looked at Ma an Pa an saw somethin I ain't seen in a long time. They was lookin at each other an smilin, an then he kissed her. I thought that was a great idea so I kissed Ruth Ann.

Everybody was real tuckered out when we turned in for the night.

Tuesday, December 26

It musta been long after midnight. Me an Peter was driftin down the Nanticoke, fishin for smallmouth bass. He had tied into one that was puttin up a good fight. Suddenly he yelled, "Get outta here!" Only it weren't Peter, it were Josiah Just screamin at someone in the next room. The walls is kind thin an I heard him scream again, "Leave us alone! Get out!" By then I had woke up all the way an figgered what was goin on, so I grabbed the Kentucky an went into the hall. I opened their door real slow an saw a big man with black curly hair standin behind Ruth Ann's mother. He had one hand on her neck an a knife in th'other.

Funny what went flashin through my head right then. I membered Kurt Johansson holdin Ruth Ann as he backed up draggin her outta his dad's store. But one big difference – Kurt was facin away from me an didn't know I was there. This guy was lookin right at me like he was darin me to do somethin.

"Drop it" he said, "now!"

Stead a droppin the Kentucky, I let it point down to the floor so's he'd keep watchin me. That way I was hopin he'd forget that Mr. Just was behind him.

I said, "Hey now, you don't wanna do somethin crazy here. There's lotsa people all over this place; you'll never get away with it."

The other thing I was hopin was that Mr. J would make some kinda move, stead a tryin for a peaceful way out. An he did. He was next to the wash stand an, smooth as silk, he picked up the water pitcher an smashed it over the guy's head. Course it was fulla water an it broke, so anyone nearby got wet. But the bad guy was done bein a bad guy. He went down hard. Mr. J took away his knife an threw it cross the room, like it was gonna bite him. I could tell swingin that water pitcher was bout as violent as he was gonna get.

He sat on the guy an said, "Levi, cut down one a them curtain drawstrings an help me tie him up, then get your Pa in here." That last part weren't needed, cause bout then Pa come bustin through the door. When he saw Mr J sittin on the crook an me usin the knife to cut some rope he said, "Oh, so that's what the yellin was all about. Levi, did you hit this guy with the rifle?"

"No Pa, Mr Just got him with the water pitcher."

"Well good for you, James. I never heard a that bein used as a weapon, but I reckon it worked!"

Through all this Mrs J had been standin in the corner, shakin an lookin real scared. So Ruth Ann took her into th'other bedroom where it was quiet an tried to calm her down.

Bout then Mr J turned to Josiah an said, "Go see if you can find Mr. Brogan. Tell him what happened and ask him to come up here. The Judge needs to know what went on but I don't want to be the one to call him."

Time Mr Brogan got there we had the crook tied up pretty good, but when Jefferson saw him he said, "What the hell! Louie, is that really you?"

Then he turned to Mr J an said, "This is Louie Gianello, one of our best chefs. Louie, why you would do something like this?"

"My wife, she need surgery real bad an I no can afford. I ask Judge for raise but he put me off. So I see people in big suite a rooms an figure they got lotsa money an jewels. I try to sneak in but they wake up, so I grab the lady. My wife, she gonna die without surgery. I don't know what else to do!"

Then Mr. Brogan said, "Well Louie, that doesn't justify attacking our guests with a knife. First I want to talk to Judge Bagley, then I'll call the sheriff. He can take your statements, Mr. Just, and decide what charges to make."

"Wait Jefferson, don't call the sheriff yet. Except for a broken water pitcher and a few scared people, no real harm was done here. Your chef is obviously desperate and the stress probably pushed him over the edge. Let's all calm down and talk to the Judge. Maybe there's a better way to deal with this than pressing criminal charges."

When the Judge got there Mr J told him what had happened. The first thing he did was ask all the Justs if they was ok, and tell them how sorry he was that such a thing happened to them in his Inn.

Then he went over to the chef and said, "Louie, I'm really disappointed in you. I know you asked for a raise but I put you off because I wanted to surprise you. I was planning to pay for your wife's surgery. Now I'm not sure what to do.

"Please Mr. Judge, don't fire me. I need this job so bad. Ama really sorry for this, but I gotta get the surgery for my Rosa an I don' know what to do!"

The Judge turned and asked, "What do you think, Mr and Mrs Just? You and your family are the injured parties. What do think I should do?"

Mr J said, "Well, like I said earlier, except for a lot of scared people, no real harm was done here. I'm sure your chef is really desperate and had run out of ideas of how to pay for his wife's surgery." Mrs J had come back in the room by then so he looked at her an said, "I'm willing to forget this whole thing. How about you, Ann?"

She said, "Can't we just back up a few hours and start over, like it never happened?"

The Judge thought for a few minutes, then he pulled himself up like he was on the bench with his black robe on, steada pajamas an a bathrobe. "Louie, go home and tell Rosa to get herself ready for the surgery. I will handle the bills. But hear this. If you ever even touch one of my guests again you'll wish you had never met me. And I'm asking everyone here not to mention this incident outside of this room."

Wednesday, December 27

Sayin goodbye this time was even harder than before, but it helped that now we was engaged. The rest a the weddin plannin would have to be done by mail. It was kinda slow, but Sarah an Ruth Ann was likely to keep the mail coaches busy for the next four months.

A New Year

Monday, January 8, 1838

Ruth Ann didn't wait very long to write to both me an Sarah. Her letter to Sarah was bout who she wanted to invite to the weddin. T'weren't a long list cause of the distance from Lansing. My letter was a lot more personal.

My dearest Levi,   *Sunday, January 2*

What a wonderful Christmas that was! I don't know how to thank Judge Bagley for all he's done for us, but I'll surely try.

I'm still up in a cloud! I can't believe we're engaged after all the fuss my Papa put up. But now he's okay with it. On the way home we had time to talk about a lot of things. Now that he knows you better he thinks we'll be very happy together and he's glad for both of us.

On Friday I was invited to a New Year's Eve prayer service and party with the youth group at our church. I met these nice young people when we moved to Lansing and they have helped me get acquainted with the community. I was sitting at a table with several of them talking about things that were going on in our lives. Of course, I showed them my beautiful ring and told them the history behind it. They wanted to know all about you and how we met and about Christmas at the Bagley Inn.

Then Kurt Johansson showed up and things went downhill fast. He came right over to our table and said, "Let's dance." I could tell he'd been drinking and I said no. I showed him the ring, said I was engaged to be married and wanted nothing to do with him, ever again,

Well, that set him off. He grabbed my arm and pulled me onto the dance floor. He said. "You ain't marryin nobody but me." I tried to push him away but I'm sure you remember how strong he is. Two of the boys we'd been sitting with at the table came over and grabbed his arms so I could get free. But when they tried to drag him off the floor he got one arm free and slammed his fist into the other boy's face. Then he turned around and took hold of me again.

Fortunately, Sheriff Lowe and his wife were among the chaperones, and he's just as big and strong as Kurt. He came over to us and put an arm-lock around Kurt's neck. He started kicking and screaming, but the three of them were able to get him off the floor and out the door. The sheriff and a deputy arrested him right there for being drunk and disorderly.

That kind of put a damper on the evening, but things lightened up at midnight when we rang in the New Year. I even kissed the two boys who had tried to rescue me. Then I kissed the sheriff -- hope you're not jealous!

The next four months are going to drag by if I can't see you before the wedding. And beside that, it will be difficult to do all the planning by mail. I know traveling is hard this time of year, but maybe the four of us could meet somewhere in between for a day. I talked to Mama and Josiah and they would be willing to accompany me. What do you and Sarah and William think?

I love you dearly, Levi.
Forever,
Ruth Ann

Monday, January 22

It's all set. Me an Ma an William an Sarah are gonna meet Ruth Ann an Mrs Just in Howell Township around middle a March. Ruth Ann's brother Josiah will come too so they ain't two women travellin alone. There's a farmer there has two rooms for rentin an we can have em both for one night.

It's bout a one day trip for us an them too, so we'll be able to spend some time that night an again the next mornin to get the weddin plans all settled.

Wednesday, January 24

Just got nother letter from Ruth Ann.

Dear Levi,   *Wednesday, January 19*

I just learned that when he came to the New Year's Eve party Kurt was out of jail on bond. He'd been charged with attempted kidnapping from that time in September when he grabbed me in the woods.

When Sheriff Lowe arrested him for drunk and disorderly conduct the judge revoked his bond and they put him back in jail. He was supposed to stand trial later this month. But Papa told me that he escaped yesterday and is still at large. But that's not going to stop us from meeting you all in Howell. If he's looking for us I'm sure he won't expect us to be there.

I can't wait to see you in March.

All my love,
Ruth Ann

I wish I was a sure of that as she is.

Rachel and Levi

Thursday, February 15

It was round seven when Ma said, "Levi, take the team an hie over to McGarrie's farm an fetch the midwife. Looks like Rachel's gonna deliver fore the night's over."

So I hitched up Mike an Maggie to the sleigh. Had a heavy snow last night so it took a while to get down to Celia McGarrie's place. Time she'd put her kids to bed an got her stuff together it was after eight so I drove the team hard. Rachel's pains was only couple minutes apart time we got back.

Ma chased all the men folk outta the house while she an Sarah helped the midwife with the birthin. I heard tell later that it was a hard one an the baby didn't start breathin right away. But Mrs McGarrie held it upside down an slapped it on the bottom til it started to cry. The yell was so loud we heard it all the way out in the barn. That's when we figgered it was ok to go back in the house.

When we walked in Sarah ran up to Matthew an hugged him. "It's a boy!" He looked like he was gonna swell up an bust. I guess every man wants a son.

They didn't let us in the birthin room to see him til after Rachel had finished the nursin an by then he was sleepin. That's when Rachel said they wanted both their kids named for her sister an brother, so they're gonna christen him Levi Broas Coons. Sarah took hold a my hand then, an I had a little trouble swallowin.

The Meeting

Monday, March 19, one month later

This past weekend just goes to prove what they say. Things don't always work out like you figger.

Oh, it started out ok. Everybody got to Howell Saturday afternoon an we settled in at the farmer's home where Mr an Mrs Kramer took in a few boarders for a weekend to make a little extra money.

After all the greetin was done (Ruth Ann an me took a little longer than the rest to say hello) we all gathered in the parlor. The first thing to get settled was the where. Both Sarah an Ruth Ann had their hearts set on gettin married at the Bagley Inn, specially since the Judge had practickly invited em.

The when weren't too hard neither. Ma said, "Rachel should have her baby bout mid-February, an oughtta be able to travel come late April or early May. If you all agree, I'll write the Judge an ask him if one a them Saturdays would be ok." Everybody agreed, so that settled the when near as we could do now.

Just then Mrs Kramer came in an said "Supper's on." We all jumped up cause we was glad for a chance to put off tacklin the who. It was likely to be the stickiest one of all. Sides, we was real hungry after all the travellin an jawin.

Mrs Kramer's a right good cook. The meal weren't fancy but everythin was fresh, right off the farm.

After supper me, William an Josiah got to talkin with Mr Kramer bout the wet summer we had an what crops to plant in spring. He had some good ideas for growin wheat an corn out in the west part a the state cause he said he grew up near Grand Rapids. The women got out their lists of weddin guests and talked bout who to invite an who not to, an that went on kinda long.

144

We was all real tired by then. Everybody settled down for the night, Ma, Mrs J, Sarah an Ruth Ann in one room, me, William an Josiah in th'other. I'd been asleep for a while when there was a knock on the door. I nearly fell, stumblin outta bed. I opened it an Mr Kramer was standin there. He told me there was a visitor down in the parlor who said he had a urgent message for me from my Pa. I guess I shoulda been suspicious, but I was still pretty groggy. I went down the stairs an as I turned into the room I had just enough time to see Kurt Johansson with his arm cocked. He slammed a big fist into my jawbone, then another to my gut. As I was goin down he chopped me on the back a the neck.

That pretty much did it. Next thing I know Mr Kramer is kneelin down with his hand on my neck, checkin to see if I'm still alive. I tried to get up but the room went round a coupla times so I sat back down an waited for it to stop. Things cleared after a few more minutes an then I membered seein that devil again. I didn't know how he found us but I spose in a small place like Lansing Township it's hard to keep secrets. I didn't really care bout that right now. I got up an stayed up. I ran upstairs with Mr K right behind me. I was so mad I didn't figger I needed the Kentucky. I was gonna kill Kurt Johansson with my bare hands. I ran toward the women's room an there he was, draggin Ruth Ann into the hall.

I guess he didn't spect me to recover so quick from the beatin he gave me cause he didn't hear me comin. I jumped him an all three of us fell to the floor. I got his arm offa Ruth Ann so she could get away an Mr K helped her back into the room. Then the real fightin started. Soon's we was standin Kurt swung hard at me. I was able to turn sideways but he still caught the side a my head and my ear really got to ringin. He came at me again with a round-house swing but I ducked it an slammed my head into his belly. I kept pushin til he went down on his back. By then I think I really did want to kill him. I sat on his chest an punched his face over an over. I didn't stop til Mr Kramer grabbed my arms an pulled me off.

He said, "That's enough, son, he's finished."

Josiah an Mr. J. tied him up hands to feet like a steer in a ropin contest. Seemed fittin too for a animal like that. The county sheriff wouldn't come til mornin so they gagged Kurt an left him layin in a closet til then. By now my hands was hurtin real bad, so Ruth Ann gently rubbed some healin lotion on em. They still hurt some, but everytime I thought bout the reason it made me smile.

Sunday mornin was church time for the Kramers so we all went along with em. By then I was feelin kinda bad bout how mad I was last night an what I wanted to do to Kurt. I told the Lord I was sorry an hoped He wouldn't let Mr Just change his mind bout Ruth Ann marryin me causa that.

On the way home Mr. Kramer stopped at the sheriff's place an asked him to come out to the farm cause a what happened last night. When he an his deputy saw Kurt they wanted to know what ran over him. Mr K pointed at me so I told em all he had done to me an Ruth Ann over the last few months.

I said, "I'm glad Mr Kramer stopped me or I mighta killed him. But now we gotta worry all over bout what he'll do if he gets outta prison again."

Then the sheriff said, "The Circuit Judge in Livingston County is real tough on repeat offenders an since this is Johansson's third, he's likely to get hard time in the county jail. But I also hear the legislature's talkin bout havin a state prison over in Jackson, an if they do, that's likely where he'll end up. An from what I hear bout other state prisons, once you're in you don't get out til the warden opens the gate." I sure hope he's right.

By then it was time for all of us to start headin back home. We'd got mosta the weddin plans pretty well settled an the ladies could do the rest by mail. Then Ruth Ann an me ducked behind the barn for a private goodbye. It gets harder ever time.

The Weddings

Friday, May 4, the day before

I can't believe it's finally gonna happen. After all the plannin an meetin an letter writin we're all here at the Inn – the Justs, the Russells an the Broas's an some a the relations. It come to bout forty folks countin the little ones. I'm not sure Judge Bagley knew what he was gettin into last Christmas when he said we was all gonna be his guests again.

They put all the men on the first floor an the women an kids on the second, an we men ain't 'lowed to go near there. Not that I'd want to! All we gotta do is get cleaned up an put on our Sunday-go-to-meetin clothes. But from all the goin's on upstairs you'd think they was expectin the Queen of England.

Tomorrow the Reverend Gordon'll hear vows spoke by the four of us. Looks like it'll be a big affair but I'm wonderin if all the fuss an bother was really necessary.

Sunday, May 6, the day after

Yesterday mornin fore the weddin Mrs J told Ma that Ruth Ann was so nervous she was up mosta Friday night. She even went outside an walked round the Inn a few times. Wish I'da known, I'da gone an walked with her cause I was wound up kinda tight too.

But the weddins came off real good. The chapel was just bout big enuff to hold everybody. Even the young'uns was there, an mostly they behaved ok, cept for little Sarah Jane who's fulla the dickens an couldn't stop talkin.

Sarah's sister Rachel an Ruth Ann's sister Margaret was the maids of honor an the two of em walked in together. Then Pa an Mr Just walked the brides up to the altar, an I never seen nothin so beautiful as those two women. When Pa handed Sarah over to William he looked at me an I could see his eyes was kinda damp,

I guess cause he was givin away two kids today. Then Mr Just gave me Ruth Ann's arm an said, "Take good care of her, Levi." "I will, Mr Just." By then me an William was bustin with pride.

After welcomin us, an sayin that he'd never done a double b'fore, the Reverend Gordon gave a talk bout families an the meanin of commitment in marriage. He asked God's blessin on our unions an then turned to William an Sarah an said, "William, repeat after me. 'I, William Russell, take you, Sarah Broas, to be my wife, to have and to hold from this day forward, for better or for worse, for richer, for poorer, in sickness and in health, to love and to cherish; from this day forward until death do us part.'"

William repeated what the Reverend said, an the rest of us each took a turn an said the same vows. Then the Reverend said, "William and Levi, you may now place the wedding rings on your brides' fingers." Williams brother John fumbled in his pockets long enuff that we started to wonder if he'd lost the ring, but then he came up with it an William put it on Sarah's finger.

Matthew weren't takin no chances – he was holdin the ring all through the ceremony, an gave it to me right quick. But Ruth Ann's hand was shakin so hard I hadta grab hold of it fore I could slip the ring on.

William an me thought that was the end of it, but the Reverend said, "At this point, Sarah an Ruth Ann asked me to read a passage from the Book of Ruth. It has an important message and is a part of many weddings:

'Entreat me not to leave you, or to return from following after you. For where you go I will go, and where you stay I will stay. Your people will be my people, and your God will be my God. And where you die, I will die and there I will be buried. '"

Then he looked out at all the people an said, "If there is anyone in this company who knows of a reason that these two couples should not be united in holy matrimony, let him speak now or forever hold his peace."

After waitin a minute he said, "Without objection, I see no reason they should not be joined. Sarah and William, I now pronounce you man and wife. Ruth Ann and Levi, I now pronounce you man and wife. William and Levi, you may kiss your brides." An we did, probly a little longer than was proper. He asked the Lord's blessin on our unions again, then said lots of nice things to us an our families.

On the way outta the chapel we got showered with rice, wheat an nuts. Coulda made a pretty good meal outta what was left on the ground.

Everybody went to the main dinin room where there was a big dinner. It was different than what Mr. Jefferson served us when we was here last spring, but it was just as good.

Then Judge Bagley told everybody how he met us an why he feels a special connection to our two families. After that Pa made a kinda naughty speech bout marriage an honeymoons that had everybody laughin out loud. I never woulda believe it if I hadn't heard him myself.

Then the dancin started. If some a them high society guests at the Inn hada been at our party they mighta frowned on it, but we was country folk an all we knew was country dancin. Everybody had a good time an that's all we cared bout.

When it got time to end the party they played a slow dance for just us two couples. Me an William finally got to hold our women real close, only now they was our wives. I felt like life couldn't get no better'n that.

But later that evenin it did.

An I ain't gonna explain why I didn't write in this journal last night!

The Honeymoon

Thursday, May 10, 1838

After the weddin ceremony Sarah an William had plans to go with Amos an Esther to Flint. Everyone else went home, but Judge Bagley invited Ruth Ann an me to stay at the Inn for a four day honeymoon. He said it woulda been longer but he had a big convention comin in tomorrow that'll take up the whole Inn

It's hard to say all that happened to Ruth Ann an me durin these four days. We got to know each other in so many new ways. We walked in the woods, we swam in the lakes, we talked an we talked -- bout our past an bout what we wanted our future to be.

An at night we brought our love to a place I never even knew existed.

Sayin goodbye to her folks that first day coulda been kinda hard cause they was goin to Lansing an she was gonna come back to Groveland with me. But it's only for a short time cause the Broas family's plannin to move to Ionia in June an we'll meet up with the Justs on the way.

On Monday we met nother honeymoon couple, George an Virginia Samson from Detroit. They showed us how to play Shuttlecock on a field behind the staff buildin. George musta played it fore cause he an Ruth Ann beat Virginia an me pretty stiff.

The Picnic

At breakfast yesterday George said, "Did you know that the Inn keeps a canoe livery on the Rouge River, just a few hundred yards south of here? Guests can use them anytime, so Virginia and I were wondering if you two would like to join us on a 'canoe – picnic'. The kitchen will even pack us a lunch."

Well, that sounded too good to refuse, so while the ladies went to ask the cook for a picnic lunch me an George found Mr. Brogan in the stable. We asked him if he had any suggestions bout the river an which way to set out.

"I'm sure you'll enjoy canoeing the Rouge. I'd suggest you start out going upstream, that's east from here, and you'll do the harder paddling while you're still fresh. Up there in the headwaters it's a beautiful stretch of clear water that cuts through some unsettled wilderness. And upstream a few miles is a nice clearing on the riverbank that's a good spot for your picnic."

"Is there any danger from Indians?" I asked. "I'm still kinda leery bout em after my run-in with some unfriendly ones last year."

"No, Levi, the few Ottawa that live in this area are quite friendly. Besides, word of your marksmanship in saving that young princess has spread throughout the tribes. You are a hero in the Ottawa nation."

By then the girls had got the lunch so me an George met up with em an we all walked down to the canoe dock. They had boats for singles an doubles an a big one for four, so we took that. It was in good shape, but it sure was heavy.

George had done lotsa canoein so he took the rear for steerin while I was the muscle up front. It was kinda tough goin at first, fightin the current. But then the river widened out an it got smoother.

After bout a hour we found the spot on the riverbank Mr Brogan told us bout an spread out the picnic lunch. It was real good – chicken sandwiches, cheese, fruit an a jug a cold tea. We was round halfway through when somethin showed up Mr Brogan didn't tell us bout – a bear cub. Now I don't think th'other three had much experience with bears, cause the women started oohin an aahin bout how cute it was. Virginia even offered it a piece a chicken.

That's when I reared up an said, "Stop! Don't never feed a bear, specially its cub. Sides, where there's one there's likely to be two, an for sure there's Mama. Real slow, people, pick up the food an let's move to the boat." Course I didn't bring the Kentucky long cause a the social nature a this outin. Sides, what would I of done with it? Shot Mama an leave two little bear cubs motherless? Or shot one a the cubs an have Mama come chargin in on us fore I could re-load? That woulda ruined the picnic for sure!

We had picked up some a the lunch when Mama an her other cub ambled outta the woods, lookin for the food they smelled. The four of us scrambled to the canoe an jumped in, almost overturnin it. George didn't need no promptin cause he was paddlin away from shore just as hard as me.

Followin her nose, Mama bear came down to the shore an started wadin into the water. Now don't let nobody tell you bears can't swim cause they can, specially if they're after somethin to eat, which in this case mighta been us. But then I guess Mama decided eatin what we couldn't pick up was easier than swimmin after a fast-movin boat, so she turned back an her an her cubs, finished our picnic.

That was yesterday. Today, me an Ruth Ann tried to thank Judge Bagley for all he done for us an our families, but it weren't easy cause he somehow feels he still owes us. When we said goodbye to George an Virginia we exchanged addresses. We gave em the Ionia post office cause we's gonna be movin next month. Then we headed for Groveland. Ruth Ann rode the horse Matthew let the Judge take after Justice was killed by the fallin tree last year. We was home fore dark.

Friday, May 11, Groveland

Course, the minute we got here last evenin everyone wanted to know what we did on our honeymoon. So we told em bout George an Virginia an the Shuttlecock games an the canoe picnic an the bears.

An that was *all* we told em.

By then Ruth Ann an me was so tired we was ready to collapse, but we didn't know where. So I asked Rachel if there was a room for us. She said, "One a the reasons Matthew an me bought this farm was cause the house had lotsa rooms. We knew folks would be comin to visit, an sides, we're plannin on havin a big family. Now, Sarah Jane an the new baby Levi have their own bedroom, an since big Sarah's gone to live with William's family, you'n Ruth Ann got your own room too. Come long an I'll show you."

Next mornin I let Ruth Ann sleep as long as she wanted. I coulda done that too, but I membered the last time I slept late here I missed breakfast an had to do the worst part a dairy farmin – cleanin the barn floor.

Back to Ionia

Saturday, May 26, two weeks later

Today we started gettin ready for the big move to Ionia County. Pa says we're gonna go there first part a June, so it's time to plan what to take an how to carry it all. We'll only have one wagon that Mike an Maggie will pull cause the oxen Matthew gave us are already out there.

Ruth Ann don't have much to take cause mosta her things is in Lansing an we'll pick em up on the way through. But me an Ma an Pa are gonna load up that wagon – clothes an sewin things an dry food an tools an feed for the horses an lotsa odds an ends. Funny how much stuff we think we can't get long without.

Saturday, June 2

The sun was just comin up when we said goodbye to Rachel an Matthew an took off for Ionia. In a way, it was like nother honeymoon. Pa an Ma was up front guidin Mike an Maggie while me an Ruth Ann was sittin together in the back a the wagon on some bags of clothes. She took my hand an said, "I've got to tell you Levi, I'm real happy but kind of scared too. Being your wife and a part of your family is wonderful, but everything is so new. And now we're going to live out in the woods where most of the other people there are Indians."

I put my arm around her and said, "I think I know how you feel, sweetheart, but trust me. As long as we're together you'll be safe, an nothin's gonna harm you. The only thing that'll matter is you an me."

She said, "I know that, Levi, and I believe you." Then she kissed me – twice.

Bout then we came onto Fenton. Pa stopped at the general store cause Ma said she forgot to bring the fennel paste an wanted him to see if they had some. Sure nuff, they did, but while he was in there he saw a headline on a copy a the Democratic Free Press. It caught him up short, so he bought one an come out an showed it to us:

Thursday, May 31, 1838

PRISON BREAK IN HOWELL

On Tuesday last a resident of Lansing Township, who was being held in the Livingston County Jail for assault and battery, escaped. He attacked a guard in the prison cafeteria with a sharpened toothbrush handle and, using him as a hostage, forced his way onto a milk delivery wagon that was leaving the property.

Three hours later the delivery man, Peter Wilson, was found unconscious alongside the Grand River Trail near Fowlerville. Wilson said later, "That madman grabbed my rifle and hit me on the head with it til everythin went black."

An alert has been issued for all of Livingston, Shiawasse and Ingham counties for Kurt Johansson. He is armed and considered very dangerous.

*   *   *

Author's Notes

This is a fictional story intended to relate the lives, accomplishments and hardships of one family that helped to settle the western portion of our state. It is based on the few facts I have about the Broas family and their relations:

- Charles Broas, his wife Catherine D. Roosa and children Peter, Sarah and Levi lived on the family farm near Binghamton NY with Charles father Peter and mother Phebe. The younger Peter died in 1836 at the age of 22.

- In 1837 Charles took his family to Michigan and stopped in Groveland, Oakland County, at the home of his daughter Rachel, her husband Matthew Coons and daughter Sarah Jane.

- Charles traveled to western Michigan with Levi, Thomas Stocking and Erastus Higbee. He established their homesite on the Flat River in 1837 or 1838 in what is now the town of Belding.

- Levi married the daughter of James Just and Ann Jane McClure. However, he and Ruth Ann were born eleven years apart and were not married until 1849. I made them closer in age because I wanted them to experience this journey together.

- Sarah Broas married William Russell, the son of Josiah Russell and Betsey Hastings, in 1840. Instead, I had them married in a double ceremony with Levi and Ruth Ann in 1838.

- There were two Abraham Roosas. One was Catherine Roosa Broas's father. The younger one, perhaps a distant relation, helped Charles and Levi build their cabin.

- Judge Amasa Bagley established Bagley Inn near the intersection of what are now Woodward Ave (the old Sagainaw Trail) and Long Lake Rd. It is the only state-designated historic structure in Bloomfield Hills.

- Seymour Finney owned a livery stable near the docks at the corner of Griswold and State that became a leading hideaway for escaping slaves.

*   *   *   *

The rest of this story is the result of conjecture and imagaination, and is not intended to represent actual people or events.

Acknowlgements

Much of the historical information on which the journal is based was obtained with the help of personnel of The Alvah N. Belding Library and the Belding Historical Museum. I am particularly indebted to Ms. Janet Hoskins, the late Mrs. Helen Salzman and the late Ms. Betty Demorest. My deepest gratitude for the privilege of knowing these wonderful ladies.

I also gleaned considerable detail from the following library and internet sources:

- U. S. Bureau of Land Management
- Wikipedia
- The Detroit News
- Grand Traverse Band of Chippewa and Ottawa Indians
- Images of Michigan
- MichiganHighways.org
- History of the Bagley Inn
- Michigan Fever
- Indians.org
- The Making of Michigan, A Pioneer Anthology
- Ancestry.com

And my sincerest thanks to –

My wife Marion for her patience and encouragement.

My daughter Lisa Mann for her constructive editing and helpful suggestions.

Carl Virgilio for his striking cover design.

The Writers Group of Shelby Township, Michigan, for all the attention and helpful comments these accomplished writers gave me, especially for Terry Hojnacki's insightful editing. Without their encouragement I might have abandoned this project in its early stages

About the Author

L. Broas Mann is a great-grandson of Levi Broas.

He was born and raised in Detroit, Michigan and obtained Mechanical Engineering degrees from Illinois Institute of Technology and Northwestern University. He was an instructor in that field at Lawrence Institute of Technology, after which he enjoyed a fifty year career as a Research Engineer and Consultant with Chrysler Corporation.

Broas and his wife Marion have four children, eight grandchildren and five great-grandchildren, and his primary interest is centered on these families. He also enjoys writing and genealogy. From many years of research, and several visits to the town of Belding, Michigan, much of the Broas family history was documented. It is this background that prompted his desire to write Levi's Journal, a fictional account of the family's journey from New York to Michigan.

Made in the USA
Charleston, SC
23 November 2013